DISNEY VILLAINS

CITY OF VILLAINS

ESTELLE LAURE

AUTUMN PUBLISHING

AUTUMN
PUBLISHING

Published in 2021
First published in the UK by Autumn Publishing
An imprint of Igloo Books Ltd
Cottage Farm, NN6 0BJ, UK
Owned by Bonnier Books
Sveavägen 56, Stockholm, Sweden
www.igloobooks.com

Autumn is an imprint of Bonnier Books UK

© 2021 Disney Enterprises, Inc. All rights reserved.

All rights reserved. No part of this publication may be
reproduced or transmitted in any form or by any means,
electronic, or mechanical, including photocopying, recording,
or by any information storage and retrieval system,
without permission in writing from the publisher.

0421 001
2 4 6 8 10 9 7 5 3 1
ISBN 978-1-83903-630-9

Printed and manufactured in the UK

For Emily van Beek, a total queen.

PROLOGUE

THE WORLD ENDED BECAUSE OF ME.

Or at least that's what I thought at first.

When I close my eyes and let myself remember the night of the Fall, it's like the ground rushes at me; it still feels like cresting the highest part of a roller coaster, then dropping down from an impossible height. Except I never got off. I can still feel myself whizzing up and down at dizzying speeds, never quite getting my feet right.

Actually, maybe I strapped into that roller coaster the day my parents and sister were murdered. Sometimes it's hard to say.

What I do know is the night the Wand – that gleaming new building, the supposed crown jewel of the Scar, the symbol of its rebirth – came tumbling down eleven years after magic died, everything changed.

Again.

Let me explain: I was fifteen.

James and I were hiding from Aunt Gia on the fire escape

1

because she constantly thought we were kissing when we weren't. We had barely gotten used to being more than friends, were just trying it on for size. But even though Aunt Gia could be easy about some things, James and me being out of her sight wasn't one of them.

No closed doors in this apartment, Mary Elizabeth. Leave the door open where I can see you. It's James Bartholomew and he is who he is.

That only made me more defiant. She should have known, even then, I wouldn't allow anyone to judge James for being a Bartholomew. James and I belonged to each other. To her, James and me loving each other so fiercely seemed dangerous. To us, after all we'd lost, it was an invitation to live, and we were answering it with a yes every second we spent together.

That night, James leaned towards me for the first time, and just as our lips met, a blue light shone so bright it blinded us and cancelled out everything else. For just a second I thought we caused it.

First there was a loud grinding noise as if the Wand were a tree being ripped from the ground by its roots, then a flash of blue so bright I saw dots for hours, and then the Wand was gone. Gone. James and I had a front-row seat for the Apocalypse, and it turned out to take all of thirty seconds.

The one-hundred-sixty-storey building disappeared on the night of its grand opening, with more than three thousand people inside. The elite of Monarch City just vanished, leaving not one trace of rubble or any kind of destruction behind. That happened.

Everything stopped working. Everything in the whole world paused.

James tightened his arms around me and pulled me back against the wall to protect me, but there wasn't any need for that. Once the building disappeared, it was just quiet, the kind you don't ever forget. Nothing moved. Not pigeons or cars or moths. Not even the air.

Aunt Gia flung open the window and made sure we were there and alive and didn't even bother with scolding us for sneaking onto the fire escape, because she was so relieved not to have yet another family member perish unexpectedly. But once she had assessed us and found us with pulses, her face was like a pancake sliding off a plate. So then we all looked.

All that was left where the building had been was a crater as neat and precise as a surgical incision.

All around us, the citizens of the Scar totally freaked out. From the fire escape, James and I watched as people who had been hanging in the neighbourhood – eating pizza, out for an evening stroll – ran down the street, screaming, waiting to be hit with pieces of building, because that's what you would expect to happen when something that size falls. But not on this night.

This was just *poof*.

It took a while before they realised nothing was going to explode or burn and that all of Monarch wasn't getting sucked into a sinkhole. Police cars came and fire engines came and ambulances came. And then they just sat there, lights flashing silently. Nothing to be done.

The news said it was a tragic anomaly. The chief and Mayor Triton made speeches, told everyone to keep calm. I guess we were lucky to be where we were, but it was right next door. We escaped it by a breath.

When the water filled the crater a few days later like blood pooling in a wound, Mayor Triton named it Miracle Lake because she had been running late to the grand opening and missed the Fall by just ten minutes. For her it was a miracle. For plenty of others, a disaster.

Funerals were held. Prayers were said. Vigils featuring votive candles abounded.

Then, when that phase of mourning was complete, things got tricky.

The Magicalists were sure the Fall was a sign we should aggressively pursue bringing back magic at all costs. The Naturalists thought it was a sign that magic itself was somehow rejecting progress, if you could call it that, sending a message it didn't want the Narrows invading the Scar and putting up all these fancy new buildings like the Wand on sacred magical ground. They believed the energies that ran beneath us were sending the Narrows a message and that if we could just do the right thing, magic would come back. The Amagicalists were sure this was a scientific phenomenon they were simply not yet able to explain, and that magic was dead and everyone needed to face the cold, hard facts.

Monarch divided into factions, each more convinced of their rightness than the next. And they fought until their passion dwindled into a dull dislike, a kind of cold war. They were always fighting anyway, but now it was all over the news and on every street corner. People searched for deeper meaning and came up empty, waiting for magic to make its triumphant return.

It didn't.

The fairies did not return, wishes remained ungranted and

dreams died by the dozen with nothing and no one to usher them along.

What's so hard to think about is what happened to all those people in the building that night. I sort of hope the people inside the Wand evaporated painlessly when it happened.

I mean, I hope that's how it works.

In case it happens again.

ONE

TWO YEARS AFTER THE FALL

SMEE WILL NOT DROP THE ISSUE OF ME SITTING shotgun on the way to school.

"No, I mean really, Cap," he's whining to James, smoothing out his leather jacket. "We should be taking turns. We live in the same house, we drive the Sea Devil together to the same place, and then I have to get out of the front seat and get in the back just so Mary can jump in front. It's—"

"Demeaning?" I suggest.

"Emasculating?" Ursula says, doing something on her phone.

"Respectful," James says. "Right."

Smee gives me a look like he's barely tolerating me and swaggers away from me so James is between us. "Just because she's your girlfriend shouldn't mean she gets to sit in the front all the time. We should take turns."

James just fixed up a classic 1968 Mustang, painted it a vintage blue, and named it the Sea Devil, and it's so gorgeous it's causing all sorts of problems. Every time he does this – finds an old clunker with good bones, tinkers with it until it drives smooth and polishes it to a high shine – Smee's inner gangster comes out. It's always kind of out anyway. He wants to be powerful, or sidekick to someone powerful at the very least. We live in a city, so I don't even know why we would be driving a car to school in traffic in the first place. We should be taking the subway, but now that's not going to happen until James abandons the Sea Devil for a new project.

Now, Ursula wedges herself next to Smee as we push our way past the crenellated white columns and through the enormous wooden doors that lead into Monarch High.

"Doofus, she is the girlfriend. You're not the girlfriend, you're just one of six annoying roommates."

"Do not speak ill of Never Land or its residents," Smee says, "or I'll make you walk the plank."

The plank is the diving board in the old pool in the old house where James and six of his friends all live. Ursula edges past a couple of Narrows dressed in their usual white shirts, loafers and jackets. We stop in front of our lockers and she gives Smee a rap on the head with her knuckle.

"Hey!" Smee says.

"Come on, you guys. It's Monday morning. We have all week to annoy each other," I say.

Monday morning at Monarch High is different from other high schools, at least from what I've heard. The Scar used to be almost all Legacy – people born with a black heart on the wrist, directly descended from magic. When I was a little kid, that was all I knew. There were maybe a few bureaucrats from Midcity, businessmen from the Narrows, but it's not like that anymore. After the Death of Magic, Legacies like my family became sitting ducks, and the Narrows – uptowners with no magic and chips on their shoulders – are like vultures, plucking up our property, forcing Legacy onto the streets and, worst of all, making us interact with their horrid offspring until they finish building them a suitable private school on land they bought cheaply from *us*. So now we have an espresso stand, a caterer who comes in to deliver lunches no Legacy can afford, and they just finished adding on a pool and world-class gym.

Legacies avoid all of it. We don't like to be bought. So now we try to stand apart. We aren't separated by jocks and geeks and metalheads and emo like I've seen on TV shows. We have separated Legacy from Narrows. Legacies wear black leather bands on our arms. We dye our hair. We dress like it's a party all the time. We wear clothes with *#LegacyLoyalty* emblazoned across the front.

But it's true, even though the school is first divided in two, it continues to divide. James and his Never Land crew – Ursula, Smee and I – act as one unit, and then there's everyone else.

James and I pause to kiss while Ursula stops to answer a call on her phone and Smee stands there waiting, hands in his pockets, watching the hall in his black-and-white-striped shirt like he's our bouncer.

Ursula slips her phone back in her pocket and says, "What glorious class have we this morning? Magical History, you say? My favourite."

"Dreena, six o'clock," Smee mutters. "Get ready for some school spirit."

As though she's heard someone speak her name, Dreena

swoops over, flanked by Lola and Casey, draped in sequin scarves, hair in two blue plaits. She's holding an armful of pamphlets.

"What do you want?" Ursula says as Dreena approaches. "Whatever you're selling, we don't need any. Although," she says, reconsidering, "if there's anything interesting you need, maybe I could get it for you? My prices are very reasonable."

"I wanted to give you guys one of these." Dreena hands each of us a pamphlet. Smee immediately drops his to the floor and looks off into space, bored. "I know you aren't political or whatever, but Lucas Attenborough's dad wants to build a mall right in the middle of town. A *mall*. They would be tearing down a whole block. We have to meet! We have to rally! This is unacceptable. We can't allow the Scar's historical district to be destroyed." Dreena would be a lot easier to take if she weren't so annoying all the time, so utterly sure of her position, sure enough to approach us even though we've worked hard to be unapproachable so we don't have to deal with people like her.

"Dree Dree," Ursula drawls, slapping her locker shut. "I like a mall as much as the next girl, but I'm on your side here. Loyalty all the way. The thing is, rallying isn't going to do any good. What you need is someone who knows what's going on in the back end. You need to find out who is paying whom and whether there might be a good reason for them to give up on their pet project." Ursula weaves in a circle around Dreena, who is paling rapidly. "Who's been sleeping with whom? Who did a naughty business deal and could be convinced to back off? That's what makes this city tick." She finishes with her mouth against Dreena's ear. Dreena shrinks like a mouse.

"But," Dreena says with less enthusiasm, watching Ursula

carefully, "it's not right! That should be enough. It's not right for them to come in here and tear down those old buildings to put in some kind of fast fashion store front."

"Maybe not." Urs pulls out her phone and starts scrolling through. "But Monarch is what it is, and you're not going to change it noodling around with sad little handmade posters. I know a few people down there. Let me know if you want me to start poking around. I could pencil you in." She smiles, her thick red lips parting hungrily. "I have next Thursday free."

Dreena lifts her nose in the air, tries to rise to a height that doesn't make her look absolutely tiny next to Urs. It doesn't work. "What would that cost? Don't people have to pay you in secrets?" she asks uncertainly.

Ursula shrugs. "Depends. I like money, too." She grins. "And favours."

"I think I'm just going to stick to the old-fashioned way," Dreena says. "Sit-ins and what have you."

"Suit yourself. Try it your way, see how far you get." Now that Dreena's made her decision clear, Ursula seems to have lost interest and searches for something in her black leather backpack.

Dreena shuffles from one foot to the other, persisting. "Our meeting is going to be at the Tea Party tomorrow if you want to come." She rustles the pile of pamphlets in her hand. "All are welcome."

"Let me know if you change your mind," Ursula says, looking up distractedly. "I'm all about making dreams and wishes come true."

Dreena, who looks like she's very much regretting her decision to come and talk to us, turns to head down the hallway. But before she can take a step, Stone Wallace goes flying across her path, into Smee, who shoves him away reflexively as we all search for the source of the fight. James steps in front of me and I get on tiptoes so I can see. Monarch High used to be a pretty mellow school. Not anymore. Not since the Narrows changed districts.

Stone is in a white T-shirt and black leather trousers with hearts pressed into the material to match the birthmark on his wrist. It looks like scales on a dangerous snake. He's usually one of the untouchable kids. He mostly hides behind the bass he plays at Wonderland, the local underage club, on weekends, and other than that keeps to himself. Apparently not today. Stone slams into Lucas Attenborough, who pushes him back easily, so Stone falls onto his back, loses his breath and looks up at us in panic. Lucas gives him a kick that's more symbolic than painful.

"Hey," James says, getting between them, Smee at his side. "That's enough." His commanding tone stops Lucas, who trains his eyes on James, striking a perfect balance between tense and utterly confident. It doesn't matter how rich or how entitled Lucas Attenborough is. He would have to be a complete moron to mess with Captain Crook, a name James half hates because the Bartholomews are a crime family he tries to distance himself from, but also uses when he has the need. And he has the need often.

Legacy kids have to take care of ourselves. Ninety-eight per cent of Legacy would rather party than fight, but with the advent of jerks like Lucas in our midst, we have to be on our game, ready for anything, all the time.

"Gawd," Justin, an outspoken Amagicalist in a plaid suit, drawls from the corner. "If everyone would just accept that magic

11

is dead, none of this would be happening. We could just move on."

His friends all nod in agreement.

"Belief in magic is the root of all of society's problems," a dour girl in pin-straight pigtails says.

Lucas sniffs, looks around the hall to see that he's totally outnumbered by Legacies, who are gathering rapidly. Flora, Fauna and Merryweather are even there, each in matching pink, blue, and green gauzy dresses, and everyone knows they have weapons on them at all times because of their falling-out with Mally Saint.

"Stone deserved it," Lucas says, staring around the hall with black eyes in challenge. "Not that any of you would ever listen to anything I say."

"No, we wouldn't," Smee agrees, giving Lucas a small shove. "Get your Narrow behind out of my hallway."

Lucas straightens his shirt with a little adjustment of his neck. "How dare you put your grimy Legacy hands on me. Do you know who I am?"

"Do I know who you are?" Smee starts doing a little boxer dance, raising his fists to eye level. "Do *I* know who *you* are? Punk. The question is do *you* know who *I* am?"

Smee looks like he's about to punch Lucas in the face, which will then lead to Lucas punching Smee in the face, which will probably mean James and the rest of his boys will jump in, so I step between them before the next terrible thing can happen. Everyone knows where this is going. If they fight, Smee will get blamed and suspended, and the rest of the Legacy kids will be impossible to control. If Lucas survives, he gets no punishment whatsoever, except maybe having to give an apology.

"Go to class, Lucas," I say, so low it's like there's only the two of us in the hallway, and not a hundred Legacy kids and him. He glances around, showing his first sign of nerves. "You're outnumbered, and if you stay and fight this fight, you're going to lose."

Lucas takes a slow look around, at all the bright colours and eyes, everyone's stance taut and ready, and he snorts in obvious disdain, letting his eyes linger over my heart birthmark, eyes blazing with hatred. "There'll be nothing left of the trash bucket you call home by the time you realise your mistake, and that's going to be a better payoff than fighting Stone… and winning." Lucas shrugs, like he's shaking off unpleasant thoughts. "I guess you're right, though. These are soft Italian leather." He looks down at Stone, who is glaring up, still clutching at his side. "I don't want to sully them." He tips his shoe upwards, puts his hands in his pockets, and as though there isn't an entire mob of Legacy kids staring at his back, he saunters down the hallway.

When the crowd disperses, Mally Saint, the coldest girl in Monarch, is calmly depositing books from her locker into her very expensive-looking leather bag. Her raven, Hellion, sits on her shoulder watching the kids disappear into their classrooms. He gives a low caw.

"Shhh, pet," she says, stroking him. Her black hair is cut into a sharp bob, and her inky clothes look like they were tailor-made from French silk draped to fit her body, which they probably were. Her black dress transitions smoothly to high-cut boots, and her signature epaulettes and double-buttoned military-style jacket make her look like she's ready for war. Her dad is rich.

Super rich. Only he's not from the Narrows uptown. He's Legacy. And as though everything and everyone is in agreement about Mally being bigger and better than everyone around her, instead of appearing on her wrist, Mally's black Legacy heart creeps from her chest up the side of her neck like a creature. She closes her locker, not a hint of stress, and looks over at us.

"Well, hi, gang," she says.

"Mally," James says.

She saunters by, Hellion watching all of us as she goes. "I would have let the boys fight," she says to me. "That would have been real entertainment." She lets a finger trail over my shoulder and I shudder in spite of myself. "That would have been... priceless."

When she vanishes round the corner a few seconds later, Ursula says, "You know, the more I think about her, the more I like her."

"You gotta be kidding," Smee says. "She's like some kind of soul sucker. Gives me the willies."

"Soul suckers can be useful when they're on your side." Ursula gives Smee another thump on the head.

"You remember when she got in a fight with Flora and them," Smee says. "I thought they were going to end up skinned."

It's true, that fight was epic. Fauna confided in me one night that Mally bossed them all around so much they decided not to invite her to their annual fairy feast to honour their fairy grandmothers. Mally took that as an act of war. She showed up at the party and stood there with her arms crossed while Hellion flew everywhere, digging his talons into the rose blossom cake, knocking over the vat of ginger beer, pecking into the chestnut-roasted suckling pig. I was at that party, and the scariest part about it was that look on Mally's face. No one would get near her because of that half smirk, but mostly it was just her cold, dark knowing. She would not be crossed lightly. But even ruining that party wasn't enough for her. Mally cut Flora's brake lines, left roadkill on Fauna's doorstep, bleached Merryweather's grass. They still don't speak. Ever. Now Mally is always alone, slipping through the hallways like some high-fashion untouchable ghost.

Anyway. Just another typical Monday morning at Monarch High. Violence. Territorialism.

It's just that lately it feels like things are getting worse.

TWO

THERE ARE THREE MORE FIGHTS BETWEEN Legacies and Narrows over the next two days. I don't think anyone knows it consciously, but I'm sure it has something to do with the fact that the thirteenth anniversary of the Death of Magic and the two-year anniversary of the Fall is coming on October 31st. A huge Acknowledgement Ceremony is planned for those who died in both cataclysms, and tensions are running high between the factions.

The wind cuts through me as soon as I emerge from the train in Midcity and walk the three blocks to the police station for my after-school internship. My stinging cheeks feel good. I like storms: rain, dark brooding clouds, umbrellas turned inside out by wind. Sometimes the Scar's relentless good weather gets on my nerves and it feels good to be in Midcity, the huge neighbourhood between the Scar and the Narrows. Here, people are paying tickets, going to corporate jobs, shopping and fighting crime, the way they do in the rest of the country. The weather changes, there's industry of one kind or another, and the streets aren't littered with lost souls, skaters and performers, like they are in the Scar.

The station is bustling with action. Nestled into one of Monarch's older buildings just over the border between the Scar and Midcity, the station has high ceilings, beige walls, white crown moulding and even some stained glass. There's something grand and beautiful about it, but what is delicate and finely crafted is overpowered by the work that's done within its walls.

Desks are clustered all throughout the enormous room, and at the far end are glass windows specifically positioned so the person in the office on the other side can keep an eye on everything that's happening in the station. That person is the chief, and as usual the blinds in her office are drawn. There's a small snack station with constant coffee brewing and baked goods, and a small pool of desks for the secretaries. That's where I am, wedged all the way into one corner so no one even remembers I'm there except the secretaries who love to hand off their boring transcribing jobs to me, and a Legacy officer named Bella whose desk is close to mine. I don't mind when they forget I'm here. It makes things so much easier. The sounds of everyone talking and the constant ringing of phones melt into one unintelligible din. Outside of the main office are smaller rooms for interrogations and private meetings, but the energy in the main space builds on itself, so I always feel that even though it's frustrating doing paperwork, at least I'm here. One step closer to my destiny.

Everyone is milling around, conversations are heated and clustered, and they all seem terribly busy. I would like to join in, to find someone to talk to who would tell me what's going on, let me in on some new and exciting case, but I know they won't. I already wasted enough days when my internship started, feeling like the five-year-old at the big-kid party, trying to be a part of important conversations and banter, and it didn't work.

I scan my badge to clock in, trying not to look as eager as I feel. It's true this is not what I had originally imagined when I trained with guns and learned how to defuse bombs, how to talk someone off a ledge and negotiate; when I learned how to get through a building safely and check all the places someone might be hiding. I was imagining I would be out on the streets of the Scar, making them safe for everyone, infiltrating spaces most others couldn't get into because I'm Legacy. I blush now, just thinking about my naivete, because it didn't stop there. I imagined myself sitting in the chief's place by eighteen, office filled with Ever roses, a medal of honour in a glass case on the wall.

No one talks to me or directs me in any way. I'm expected to come in, sit at my desk, do as much as I can, then leave without making a fuss. What I've learned since I began this internship is that, although it isn't at all what I thought it would be, I'm *here*. I've taken one step towards the thing I want. It's just going to take me a lot longer to get where I want to get than I originally thought.

I'm not like so many of the detectives and officers milling about in here, though, hands on their guns, thickening at the middle, droopy eyes – beaten.

And also, there's another thing I can only sometimes admit to myself. The afternoons I'm here, I'm closer to the chief than I have been since all those years ago when she solved my family's murder, when she and Mayor Triton each held one of my hands at the press conference. She strides by with her assistant following behind and a constant entourage of people vying for her attention while I watch her from a distance.

Someday, she will see me.

I think.

Actually, probably not.

Jeanette, one of the secretaries, comes by and deposits another folder on top of my pile. "I have another Mad Hatter report for you," she says. Jeanette has two kids at home and I'm pretty sure she feels sorry for me. "You should do this one first. And put it back *you know where* when you're done reading." She taps the folder. "Body parts in boxes. Doesn't get much better than that."

It's been going on since just before I started here. Body parts showing up all over the Scar, which is of special interest to me because everything that happens in the Scar is interesting to me. So far there's been a thigh, an arm, a hand with the fingerprints cut from the skin. They all seem to belong to the same person, and they come in these boxes wrapped up like Christmas gifts, frozen in dry ice. Studying this case is my afternoon dessert.

"Thank you," I say.

She winks at me and moves on, smoothing out her grey skirt as she goes. "You're welcome, sweetheart," she says.

I can hardly wait for her to be gone before I open the file. I'm faced with pictures so grotesque they should make me throw up, but they don't. They interest me. This would make even Ursula gasp. It's on par with something Mally would do on her very worst day. And it's so compelling. I know I'm just supposed to transcribe reports and then file them, but times like these

I wonder if there's another way for me. A more exciting way. Maybe I could forge one from nothing.

I breathe deeply, and then when I have it together again and the room has stopped its dizzying kaleidoscope and my mind has stopped thinking all its treacherous thoughts, I carefully set the file aside. I will come back to it when I have time to sink into its contents, and revel.

THREE

BY NEARLY SIX O'CLOCK THE STATION HAS
calmed. The daytime shift has gone home, the night-time
shift is on the street, and patrols are up so there aren't as many
uniformed officers in the building. There's a lazy intensity in
those who are left. Phones ring sporadically, a few officers have
interrogations going on inside rooms, and the rest seem to be
researching and typing.

I should be off, home or with James or at Wonderland, but
instead I've transferred my in-tray to the floor next to my desk
so I have more room to lay out photos and one of the giant maps
of Monarch the detectives keep rolled up in a basket. This one
is battered and faded, but it'll do. I've marked it with a pencil
everywhere the gift-wrapped body-part boxes have appeared.
I examine the pictures of the cards that have come with the
packages, the curlicue writing, the distinctive black ink that
almost looks like it's still wet, like it came from a fountain pen.

> With Love,
> Mad Hatter

What does he want? I take a pencil and draw lines connecting each location and then sit back.

Interesting… all the locations seem to be in places that are meaningful to the Magicalists. Outside the Ever Garden, where flowers bloom all year long, the Lower Monarch Bridge, where the Magic March took place ten years ago, and in front of the Wand Emporium, which got taken down just after the fairy godmother craze, located as rumour would have it over a huge bed of crystals that some say is the source of magic itself. The person doing this has to be from the Scar. But why? Is it some kind of threat to its citizens? Some Amagicalist trying to send a message?

I hear the sound of throat-clearing and pop out of my cocoon, alarmed. This is technically a confidential file Jeanette shared with me, which she's done a couple of times to keep me from total boredom and despair. I'm so used to going unnoticed I'm not being as discreet as I should. I cover the map and file protectively, then realise who it is.

Bella Loyola, a young officer who is also the only other Legacy in the building besides the chief, sits across from me, arms crossed, one eyebrow raised from behind her horn-rimmed glasses. In a vest, white buttoned shirt and plaid trousers, she looks every bit the bookish Goody Two-shoes she is, even though I have to admit she is stylish in the way she does it. And that hair? Dark brown and lush, thrown into a messy ponytail it's easy to see took her half a morning to get just right.

She smiles warmly at me, giving me a little reprimanding look. "Confidential?" she mouths, pointing to my desk with one finger, which she then turns into a light wag.

I shouldn't be surprised. She's pointed out things I'm doing wrong before. I think she might be trying to be helpful in a big-sisterly way, but I don't like feeling that I have to answer to her. She even corrected the way I made the coffee once, gently informing me the detectives don't like it too strong because they drink it constantly. She's barely above me in the station hierarchy. As far as I'm concerned, there's only really one person who can tell me what to do, and it's not Bella.

I wave at her like I didn't understand and then point over her shoulder. Tony, her partner, is approaching from behind her. Our eyes meet for a brief moment before she turns her attention to him.

"You ready to go get a bite to eat from downstairs?" he says.

"Oh," Bella says, "uh, actually I'm working on the report from the Narrows case we covered yesterday. I don't want to get too behind on all that." She smiles at him.

"No no no," he says, laying a hand over her folder. "We should go. You need to learn to relax. You're wound up so tight."

She pulls the folder from under his elbow. "You go on," she says.

"Uh, Officer Loyola," I say, "can you help me with something?"

Tony looks over at me. "She's trying to take a break."

"I just need a second."

"She's new. I'm going to help her. Go to dinner, Tony."

He stands and stretches, overpowering the space with his weirdly developed shoulders. "Fine," he says, "but one of these days you're going to come sit down for a real meal with me."

Bella gives him a small smile then comes over to my desk.

"What do you need?"

When Tony's gone she says, "Thank you," under her breath, and then she goes back to her desk and stares straight down at her paperwork. I may be wrong, but I think I see tears welling up.

I go back to my file without saying anything. I know that feeling of frustration and anger at not being able to say something you really want to say. I also know that no one wants to be watched when they're trying to recover from it.

I try to focus on the Mad Hatter again, and before I know it, I'm sucked in. I hope the person who's been chopped up was a really bad person, deserving of this punishment. Because I think bad people should have this end. I think if you hurt someone, you should be hurt.

I flash on my parents as I saw them that day, and my sister when I accidentally caught sight of the crime scene photos, all that blood. There was no mercy for them and there should be no mercy for Jake Castor, either, the predator who took their lives while I was at school. He said he just wanted to know what it would feel like to take lives. He had been tracking my mother's comings and goings for days and when she was likely to be home. It was both random and planned. He didn't know my sister or my dad would be there, both sick and home unexpectedly. He said, when he finally admitted everything, that he panicked when he saw there were three people in the apartment instead of one, but he knew he would be able to overpower them because they were Legacy, and Legacies without magic are sitting ducks.

And he was right.

The idea that he's languishing in some prison instead of in pieces makes me so furious, I have to concentrate to get my cheeks to stop flaming. But I guess that's better than the alternative – that he's still out there. I have the chief to thank for that.

I comfort myself, thinking someday I'll be the one bringing people to justice, making the Scar a safe place to live again. I might even be able to unify everyone. I picture myself waving from a float, a ticker-tape parade, throngs of people worshipping me, thanking me for saving the city.

My reverie is interrupted as someone speaks in a low but certain baritone that carries across the space and sends shivers all through me. "Get your hands off of me," the voice says, calm in spite of the words themselves. "I will see the chief immediately."

"You can't see her, sir," a female officer says in a nasal voice, obviously incredulous at his tone. "She isn't taking visitors today. And there's a no-pet policy here. Unless it's one of our K-9 unit, and that is not one of our K-9 unit, you're going to have to leave and come back without that…"

The bird on the man's shoulder, sleek and inky, snaps at the officer's pointed finger, and she withdraws it and steps back as the man caresses the bird's head, slipping something from his pocket into its beak. "Hellion," he says, "we'll find her."

"That's Mally Saint's dad," I murmur, realising it as I say it. And that's Mally Saint's bird. I've never seen Hellion anywhere but on Mally's shoulder, his shining eyes enough to keep everyone at a distance from her. Apparently, he's an emotional support bird Mally got after her mother died in the Fall. At least that's what she says. More like a guard bird.

Bella, who has been taking notes on something, has a pencil

25

dangling from her mouth, and she's so engrossed in watching what's happening she tries to speak with the pencil still between her lips. It comes out gibberish. She pulls out the pencil, glances my way, and whispers, "You know Jack Saint?"

Jack Saint.

"No," I say. "Only his daughter."

"Ah," Jack says, when the door to the chief's office swings open. "There she is. *La Grande Dame.*"

The chief strides out of her office and my breath catches, along with everyone else in the station. She's dazzling in a cream-coloured suit, tailored to her thin body, her signature stilettos clicking as she travels the distance between them. "It's all right," she says to the officers following closely after her. "I can handle him."

"Ma'am." One of the officers hesitates and the chief waves him away.

"I told you I'm fine. This is an old friend of mine."

"Charlene," Jack Saint says, his body relaxing slightly at the sight of her. He is so tall and so thin, his grace is surprising. He moves like a crooked shadow, every feature so pointy any one of them could cut glass. But even from here I can tell his eyes are warm and sad, the gentle blue of island beach water in a magazine. He bends to kiss the cheek the chief has offered him. Hellion repositions himself.

Meanwhile, Bella is leaning precariously out of her chair as she watches them with rapt attention, focusing on every word.

"You're going to fall over," I whisper.

She waves me off like I'm going to make her miss something with my talking, but then she does nearly slip off the chair and rights herself with a quick glance and half smile in my direction.

And we must have missed something, because now they're sitting down and the chief seems to be answering a question.

"I'm going to do precisely what I always do," the chief says. "I'm going to do my job."

The station is silent, all eyes on Jack Saint and the chief.

"Last night, Hellion came home without Mally," Jack says. "He came home upset." He thrusts his phone in the chief's face and she looks without moving. "She calls me every single day at two forty-five p.m. on the dot to tell me of her plans, and yesterday she did not, and then Hellion..." His voice catches. "She is *never* without Hellion." He stops and composes himself. "We have agreements since her mother died. She never breaks those agreements. I have been trying to go through the proper channels, trying to get help, but no one will listen to me. Something has happened to my daughter and I want you to find her and bring her back."

"Jack," the chief says soothingly, running a hand along the back of his suit, "it's only been a day. Give it time. She's a teenager. Everything will be fine. I know it's been difficult since you lost Marion."

"She's all I have left," Jack says, taking the chief's hand and gazing deep into her eyes. "She's everything."

Hellion makes a cooing noise and pecks gently at Jack's ear.

For a moment it's as though Jack and the chief are somewhere together, alone, not in a station at all. No phones ring. No one types or speaks. The station is utterly silent. When Jack finally breaks eye contact and ducks his head, it's like he's a great dinosaur bird and not a man at all. "What happened to her, Charlene?" he says. "Is someone holding her prisoner? Monarch has become so unruly and dangerous, and we have luxury while many do not. Her behaviour has been less than ideal." He hesitates. "She's made enemies. And if she's wounded and there's no one to help her?" He lets his head fall onto his hands. "What would become of me? It has only been one day, it's true, but I know my daughter and she would not do this. They say the first forty-eight hours are the most important. Please, Charlene. I am a lonely man, living in a tower, and I have but one thing I care about. One. And she is in danger."

Hellion caws and stares at the chief as though daring her not to take Jack's plea seriously.

Jack reaches into his inside coat pocket and pulls out a picture. He places it on the table and slides it over the wood, closing the small space between them. "Mally," he says, tapping the picture. "She doesn't care for anywhere but here. Monarch. She wouldn't leave it by choice."

The chief sits up straight, reaches for his cheek. "I'm going to do my best to help you find her. You have my word. She will come back," the chief says, firmly.

This sends a thrill through me. The newspaper articles I've read say that when it came to the murder of my parents, she was like a dog with a bone, that she wouldn't stop until she had solved the case, even when it ran cold and seemed there would never be an answer.

The certainty in her voice seems to have the same effect on Jack as it does me.

For the first time since he burst into the room, Jack Saint seems to calm; only the bird on his shoulder is agitated. "You think that the Great Death ended magic and that the Troubles are over, but there are those who hold ill will."

The chief flinches the tiniest bit, then nods to one of the officers who has been standing nearby, waiting for the sign. "Goodnight, Jack. We'll be in touch. Meanwhile please go with Officer Henshaw. He'll help you fill out the relevant forms."

Jack Saint allows himself to be guided towards the door. He stops and gives the chief a hound-dog stare. "Forget our past. Forget the Troubles. Just please help me find Mally."

"Of course, Jack," the chief murmurs, then she rises and glides across the floor, into her office, leaving the door open.

No one moves until the chief's secretary, Mona, who has been off to the side with her clipboard, says, "All right, now. Everyone back to work." Then she disappears inside the office and closes the door firmly.

The second she's gone, a slew of gossipy conversations start up among those left in the station.

I try not to crane my neck, but I want to see what's happening behind the glass walls of the chief's office. The blinds are down, but I can feel the intrigue seeping from the bottom of her door. Bella and I share a look, and then she pushes her glasses back up her nose and flips open a file, crossing her legs and letting one bounce, pretending she's not as interested as me.

I try to focus on the Mad Hatter again, but the words and locations swim across the page nonsensically.

Mally is missing.

I just saw her at school yesterday.

She was fine.

I can't imagine anyone approaching her or taking her off the street successfully. From everything I know about Mally, she would tear someone to pieces before she would ever allow herself to be hurt. And Hellion? How did anyone get past him?

I roll up the map and surreptitiously drop the file onto Jeanette's desk, and then go back to my dull filing. At least then my thoughts about Mally can roam freely. I try to think about where I usually see her. She slinks around Wonderland a lot, not talking to anyone, never dancing. She lurks around the halls at Monarch High. Other than that, I never see her except when her limo rolls in and out of the school car park like some giant black snake. I've got used to her, to the grudging respect she shows James and Ursula and me. If something terrible could happen to her, why not us?

But would Flora or Fauna or Merryweather take vengeance on her? They carry knives. Maybe they aren't the pastel sweethearts they seem. Maybe they're capable of worse than she is.

After a few minutes with people going in and out of the chief's office, the door opens and Mona bursts out.

Mona bursts everywhere. She is always in a hurry and has a nurturing way about her, but also lacks patience and sometimes seems as if she'd like to box a few ears. She's been here for more than twenty years and was assistant to the chief before this one. Within days of starting my internship it became obvious the whole place would fall to pieces without her. I can't even imagine what it would be like to walk in here and not see her in one monochromatic outfit or the next. Today she's in an emerald-green blouse and forest-green skirt. Large green beads flank her throat, and two jade hoops decorate her ears. She fusses with her clipboard then peers around the room.

"Oh, good," she says when she sees Bella. "You. The chief would like to speak with you."

My stomach flops in on itself with envy and I feel my face reddening as Bella stands. She looks around and says, "Me?"

Mona nods an affirmative and scans the room again. "And you." She points and everyone turns to look. "Yes. You!" She looks down at her clipboard, then back up. "Mary Elizabeth Heart, correct?"

Me. She's pointing at *me*.

"Well, why are you sitting there like a bag of sand? Come on!" She motions again and a whole new set of internal gymnastics gets under way. I have to tell myself to calm down, to get a grip, to be professional, competent, unemotional, but all the blood in my body is rushing around so fast I feel like I'm about to combust.

Bella waits for me and we cross into the chief's office together. As I step through the doorway, I trade in the smell of coffee and paper for that of a pleasant musky perfume. The inside of the office is all hard angles, lots of white. There are no plants except a lone cactus near the one window looking out onto city rooftops. Rain splats against the glass. The room would feel empty except for the walls, which are absolutely plastered in photographs and awards.

Bella, who is already seated in one of the chairs, looks startled when I thump down next to her. She's leaned forward, hands fidgeting in her lap. I'm trying to be graceful, I swear, but in this room I feel bulky and clumsy and dirty. I focus on the chief, who scans us both. I take the opportunity to scan her back. The closest I've been to her since I was a kid is when I opened the letter inviting me to intern on the Monarch Murder Squad.

Up close, the chief is as regal as she is from a distance, with bones like a deer and pin-straight black hair. Her nails are painted red, makeup precise and designed to complement her Japanese features to great effect. She's stunning and somehow frightening at the same time.

I half expect to find a picture of us on the wall like the one that's on my own: us at that famous press conference, me holding on to her leg as she shields my face from reporters, but there's nothing there. She has solved so many murders, my story is probably nothing to her. The chief has been in the middle of every criminal investigation for ten years. No, not in the middle. In charge of.

Pictures of her shaking the president's hand.

Of her with Monarch's own prize boxer.

With the city council.

The mayor.

With everyone's favourite actor.

At press conference after press conference, in front of microphones.

"Well," she says, jolting me back to reality with her smooth but steely voice. "Ghosts forbid my blood pressure should ever descend to non-threatening levels." She nudges at the glass in front of her, and Mona immediately materialises with two more glasses and a pitcher of water, and fills all three, offering to Bella and to me.

I take a sip of the water. It's the perfect temperature, cool and inviting, and I realise I'm parched.

The chief slides a picture of Mally Saint across the desk towards us. School pictures, even when they're decent, always seem a little creepy, especially when they show up on a missing poster or a news story, but this one stirs something else in me. The cruelty with which Mally stares into the camera is breathtaking in its intensity. Her generous mouth is reddened, black lines her narrowed eyes, and her black hair points down sharply, but more than that, her eyes declare war on the world and everything in it.

Chief Ito exhales and looks from me to Bella. "The Scar. Ten square blocks. You would think it wouldn't be as much trouble as it is. And yet…" She makes a steeple of her fingers. "It used to be called Wonder." She looks between us. Of course we know this. They renamed it the Scar after the Midcity Riot, to acknowledge the wound left by all those deaths. "Sometimes I think renaming it is the source of the problems we face today. The Scar is so much darker, don't you think?"

"Ma'am," I say, because some response seems required.

"How many in that high school these days?"

It takes me a second to realise she's talking to me.

"I believe it's about fifteen hundred, ma'am."

She nods. "We used to have more, but so many people have left the Scar now. You know Mally?"

"No, ma'am," Bella says. "Although I know of her. She has been known to ride around in a limousine. Makes a person stand out in the Scar, ma'am."

"I'm sure it does. Mary Elizabeth?" the chief says. "Anything to add about Mally Saint?"

"No, ma'am. I only know her from across the room," I say, then add, "We are often in the same room."

"I hadn't seen Jack Saint in many years." The chief seems not to have heard what I said. "It took me back, was… unexpected. I

33

went to Monarch High, you know, and I hadn't… Well, that was another life, wasn't it?"

"You went to high school in the Scar?" I blurt. I figured she had been shipped off to some important boarding school in Switzerland or something. I can't imagine her dealing with those long hallways and boring classes.

"I did go to Monarch High, although it's hard to remember now. It was so very long ago." The chief runs her index finger across her forehead and searches my eyes. "So now this," the chief says. "The Scar at the centre of everything again."

"Ma'am?" Bella says after the chief is silent for a few moments, seemingly lost in memory.

"My apologies." The chief refocuses on us, opening a file folder and turning it so we can see its contents. Even from where I sit I can see Merryweather Holiday's name listed. They did file a report when Mally cut the brake lines. "Mally Saint has gone missing and I know of at least three people who would say that's a good thing. And you're exactly right, Bella. People in the Scar are… resentful, shall we say, of people of means. That, too, is problematic in this situation." She sighs. "The point is, I wouldn't normally focus on something like this, but with everything that's going on right now, with this Mad Hatter situation and the shenanigans that are positively *infiltrating* this town despite my best efforts to date…" She tightens her jaw. "The last thing I need is drama over a girl who's probably in a hotel room with someone she met in some club last Saturday night, picking up parasites from the questionable bed linens."

We sit, waiting. I wouldn't dare interrupt her, even though the likelihood of Mally Saint softening up long enough to go anywhere with anyone these days is slim to none, never mind kissing or doing anything at all on a bed. I can hardly imagine her thawing long enough to sleep.

"Now," she says, "I'm told you're excellent at finding things, Mary Elizabeth."

"I haven't done anything except find a few sets of keys, someone's lost lunch…"

"Never argue with someone who is pointing out a truth. Humility is unnecessary." The chief straightens her jacket as though my words have wrinkled it. "It's also tiresome."

"Yes, ma'am, I am good at finding things."

"Not surprising. You're Legacy. I believe in Traces."

Traces. Hints of what we once were or would have been if magic hadn't expired.

"Yes, ma'am."

She turns her attention. "And you, Bella, are good at solving puzzles. Mally was last seen at the…" Here she looks to Mona.

"Wonderland," Mona offers after consulting her clipboard again.

"Right. That dump."

I try not to take that personally. Aside from the fact that my boyfriend and best friend would be a lot happier if I were there right now, Wonderland is where I spend most nights and weekends. I hold the croquet pinball record, and it's the only place in the Scar where we can hang out and listen to live music or whatever. Plus the owner, Dally Star, is a friend.

My palms are sweating.

"For the purposes of finding Mally Saint, I'm reassigning you to each other." The chief straightens the papers on her desk to punctuate her statements. "After that, I'll reassess. I think you're going to be of vital importance here, Mary Elizabeth."

Bella looks at me, then back to the chief. "Excuse me, ma'am, but does that mean I'm no longer assigned to work with Officer Gaston?"

Chief Ito pauses and says, "It does."

"Well," Bella says, brightening. "I suppose it's not all bad."

"What's that supposed to mean?" I say before I can stop myself.

"Oh, dear," Mona says.

"Oh, nothing," Bella says, patting my hand. "No offence intended. It's just you're an intern, and you're seventeen."

"And you're what? Twenty-one, tops?"

"Ladies," Chief Ito says.

We both remember where we are and stop arguing. I'm nearly breathless with indignation, but I fight to calm myself down.

The chief stares at both of us sharply. "Mary Elizabeth won this internship with her skill and insight, and I'm going to need you to trust my judgement. I think I've earned that, don't you?"

Bella nods. "Yes, ma'am. Of course, ma'am."

"You'll have to learn to get along. It's something I've been considering for some time now, and this gives us the perfect opportunity. The Scar needs more support than the force on the street can provide, and we all know they aren't going to take it from outsiders. I'm hoping if they feel your presence, perhaps more Scar citizens will want to join up and serve in their beloved neighbourhood. They need detectives present and attending to their issues. The Scar has become too insular. It has created a vigilante climate. I can't have that. You should look at this as a unique opportunity. I don't need to tell you both the doors that will open to you should this be a successful endeavour." She puts up her hand as though to stay any further discussion. "It's decided."

She glances at her watch, then back at us.

"You need to refresh. Get food. Bathe. Come back when you're done with your morning classes tomorrow, Mary Elizabeth. In the meantime the first course of action will be to—"

"—interview the students whose parents have already filed reports against Mally," Bella finishes. "Merryweather Holiday, Flora Honeydew and Fauna Redwood are the girls in question…" She looks as though she's startled herself by speaking. "I believe."

"Yes," the chief says, looking impressed.

I feel another spike of envy.

"I read the reports months ago, ma'am," Bella says with a humility-ridden, bashful smile. "Something of a photographic memory, you see."

"Very good," the chief says. She takes her time answering, tapping her pen against the desk. "You think I am oblivious in here, but I am paying attention." She looks at me directly. "I know about your little forays into the confidential files." Her eyes are such a dark brown they appear black. "I know everything. Don't forget it." She finally releases me, looking down. "Mona, give them the files." She looks at Bella. "And meanwhile you can acclimate yourself to this new partnership. I expect to hear about nothing but blissful union between you from this point forward. You will be the lead, of course, but not to Mary Elizabeth's exclusion."

Mona hands Bella the manila files as we stand.

"I know you won't disappoint me," Chief Ito says.

37

"Of course not, ma'am," Bella says before I can.

"Because if you do…"

She doesn't need to finish her sentence and she doesn't. Because if we do disappoint her, we won't get another chance like this again. Bella will go back to the bottom, and I can kiss the chance for this internship to turn into a real job once I graduate goodbye.

"You may go," she says.

Bella and I stand.

"Not you, Mary Elizabeth. I'd like a word."

Bella backs out as the chief faces the flicker of the computer screen and sifts through the ten thousand emails that have probably been popping up in the minutes we've stolen, while Mona is organising herself at a small desk in the corner.

"How's your therapy going?" Chief Ito says without looking at me. "With Dr Tink?"

"It's good," I say, not wanting to show my surprise. She really does know everything.

"That's good. I'll need you to be in top shape if you're going to be doing real police work, so you'll need to keep up with those appointments. This is not for the faint of heart."

"I know. I… I want to thank you for this opportunity. I will make you proud, I promise." I'm stammering and can't control it. "I… I value what you've done for the city… You're… amazing. My parents." I say the words I've wanted to say since the day I set foot in the building. These words might be the very reason I'm here at all. "My sister, Mirana."

"Yes." It's clear she's trying to put me out of my misery by shutting me up. "I know. I'm glad we were able to solve it."

"There wasn't any we. *You* solved it," I say, wishing I could keep the passion from my voice. "Extra time, independently. Everyone else had forgotten."

"My boss certainly wasn't happy..." She smiles, remembering something.

"But you didn't give up even when they pulled you from the case."

She nods, seems embarrassed. "I don't like cold cases. They don't sit right with me."

"Nights, weekends. You put yourself in danger to catch Jake Castor and bring him to justice. You're my inspiration. For everything in life. I... I just want you to know that. I promise you I will make you proud."

I wait as the seconds stretch into a long minute. She leans back in her chair, and I can see she needs a day off, an eye mask and some Oreos, maybe six episodes of *Love Island* to forget what weighs her down.

"I've spent quite a lot of time with your file, Miss Heart." She folds her hands on her desk while I wonder if I should fill the silence. But then she goes on. "I'll be honest, I had to think through whether a person such as yourself, with your level of trauma, could be trusted, whether a job like this with its constant attendant pressure would be a boon to your abilities or a detriment. And with the loss of your family, I know it must have been the natural reaction to keep people at bay, to stay within the confines of the Scar, its ten square blocks. No one knows them better than I. You're a prodigy, Mary Elizabeth, with all the makings of a fine detective, or I never would have approved your internship placement here, no matter your test scores or your physical capabilities." She meets my eyes, evenly.

"The trouble with Legacy is they put Legacy before anyone else, always. Legacy Loyalty, as the saying goes. They are unruly, unkempt and more concerned with personal freedom than justice. Without magic to focus them, they are unbridled chaos and unchecked emotion. And I say that as one of them... one of *you*." She tugs at the white blouse at her wrist so her black heart is visible. I have always known the chief was Legacy, but this is the first time I've seen it. My hand goes reflexively to my own and lingers there. "You're going to earn your place here or lose it. And part of that is understanding that we're a family. You'll be in the trenches with people, and they need to know they come before the Scar and magic and the Troubles... all of it. In the end we're here for one another because no one else will be. The question is whether you will realise that or simply fade into Scar alleyways and live a small and tired life, trapped in what once was. It is Wonder no more. You can avoid the second option if you so choose. The whole world could be yours."

I swallow and nod. "Ma'am," is all I can manage.

"I'm sorry about your family, Mary Elizabeth," she says as she goes back to her computer and places her reading glasses on her nose. "Now go find me that girl, preferably alive. Use your uncanny street smarts to bring me my prize. And remember, with a job like this, you have the opportunity to keep what happened to you from happening to others."

I'm about to tell her again that she can rely on me, that I would rather lose my life than disappoint her, when Officer Laslo pushes the door open.

"Yes?" the chief says, then her breath catches.

"Another box, ma'am. We already checked it, but we thought

we should bring it to you right away. It... it was addressed to you."

The chief stands. "Put it down and open it."

"But—"

"Now."

Officer Laslo places the box on the desk, moves its opulent red satin ribbon out of the way and lifts the top.

A hand rests in the centre, mist rising all around it as the dry ice burns off. Its fingernails are blackened, and congealed blood crusts at the wrist. It's discoloured grey, and the middle finger is pointed straight upwards, swearing at the chief.

She blanches as Mona comes around to usher me out. "Shoo, dear," she says, nudging me over the threshold and out the door, where Bella is waiting for me, hardly able to contain her questions.

FOUR

WHEN WE GET ONTO THE STREET, BELLA AND I
face each other awkwardly. Other than a couple of street lamps,
it's dark. Aside from the cathedral-like design of the station
itself, all the architecture in this area is tall and rectangular, and
casts off an aubergine-purple colour in the absence of light. The
rain has stopped, but it's still cold and the wind zips through the
corridors between buildings. I never feel comfortable anywhere
around here. The trees are so manicured and equally spaced,
with raised flower beds on even-numbered street corners. In the
Scar there are palm trees, and flowers grow wild. Without the
literal warmth of the Scar and the constant hum of people and
revelry on the streets, everywhere else feels lacking and devoid
of spirit.

I zip up my coat and adjust my backpack. I don't think either
of us knows what to say. We're probably both heading to the Scar,
but I'm going to Wonderland and I don't want her coming with
me. For one thing, she seems like she might be an irritation, but

also I want to go down there and get as much information about Mally as I can on my own. I know we're supposed to be partners and it shouldn't be a competition, but it is. Best I acknowledge that to myself now. If I can find Mally without anyone's help, I'm almost sure to get a real position when my internship is finished. There's also the small matter that I don't want her to see me squealing and jumping up and down, because I can't wait to get to my friends so I can tell them I'M ON A REAL CASE! Of course I won't be able to tell them what it is, but that's okay. I'M STILL ON A REAL CASE!

"You taking the train?" I ask, betraying no signs of my internal delirium.

"I am." She clutches the manila files Mona gave her to her chest. I would love to snatch them from her. "Shall we walk together?"

"Sure."

"Listen," she says as we descend the hill to the station. "I want you to know that I'm here for you if you have any questions."

"Questions?"

"Yes, about procedure, rules, anything about the case."

I try to keep my voice sounding light, but I'm bristling over her tone. "I think I'm good. Can't wait to have a meeting so we can brainstorm strategy. I have some ideas."

"I just want to make sure you're planning to do this by the book."

"What's that supposed to mean?"

"Well," she says, still moving ahead at full steam in those adorable little Oxford loafers, "from what I've observed you don't always follow the rules, and since this is my first time as lead, I want to make sure no one has cause to reprimand us."

"Okay?"

"So no more stealing confidential files—"

"I didn't steal them. And I would never betray the chief or anyone else on the force."

"No," she says, "I suspect you wouldn't. Still. By the book. And like I said, I'd be happy to go over what that means."

"No thank you," I say. "Like I said, I'm good." I realise this is a smidge hypocritical, considering the thoughts I was just having, but what she's saying to me is just plain insulting, and I'll be damned if I'm going to have her shadowing me the whole time, looking over my shoulder and acting so superior. That's the kind of thing that will send me over the edge very quickly. I can see the train station from here and I'm not in the mood for giving her any more of my time. "Bella," I say, "let's just get everything out in the open right now. I may be seventeen, but I'm Scar seventeen, not idiot Narrows seventeen. Let's remember what that means."

We pause before we get to Mission Avenue, where there are far more people around. Bella puts a hand on her hip and looks at me with one eyebrow raised. "Go on," she says.

"It means I've lost everything once already and I have no illusions about life. It means I don't care about anything except doing this job so when I get out of high school I can actually have a life and take care of myself and my aunt. Just understand one thing: I'm not *beneath* you. So let's work together and make a name for ourselves. Because I don't know about you, but I am probably as sick of filing as you are of being the girl trailing behind Tony."

Bella seems to think about this and then nods tightly.

"Well, then, let's totally destroy this case," I say.

"Destroy?"

"Yes. Let's solve it and then solve another and another until they give us all the awards and all the accolades and no one can ever tell us anything except 'thank you' ever again."

I don't know if I even mean what I've said, but it feels good to let some of the excitement I feel about our case bubble to the surface.

"Yes," she says, her voice matching mine. "I like that idea. Let's do that. Can you even imagine what they would say? Two girls from the Scar positively dominating the force!"

"The chief would be so proud of us."

"The guys on the force would have to give us respect!" She slips an arm around my shoulder.

"We might get to be on TV!"

"We might get to *run* a press conference!"

"Yes!"

We're both giddy and smiling and lost in our own imaginings when we start walking again. I'm in lock step with her.

Her laugh is throatier and fuller than I would have expected, and I have the same lurching feeling I always do when I have found something I was looking for.

FIVE

HOME SWEET WONDERLAND. HOW I MISSED YOU.

There are so many people here from school you would never think it's a weeknight if you just walked in for the first time. Probably in any normal place kids would be at home doing healthy home things. But not here. This is the Scar, where everyone parties like it's the end of the world, mostly because we already survived it. What else are we to do with our restless bones?

I search automatically for Mally Saint and find she isn't in her usual place on the dais. There was a small part of me that was hoping maybe she would be up there like a storm cloud with Hellion on her shoulder, but part of me is also glad she isn't. I don't want her to be dead or anything, but I do want to be the one who finds her and brings her home.

There are only three tables up there, and two of them are currently occupied by Lucas and Katy. Katy is in a pink midi dress, hair in a styled bob, and Lucas in his usual coat and tie, buttoned shirt, with his brown hair slicked back. They pay heavily to have that table, but no matter how much Dally Star bumps the price so they'll leave, they continue to pay it. I'm sure Lucas Attenborough wouldn't allow himself to move among the riff-raff. In fact, I think he comes here for the sole purpose of feeling superior and talking about us from the safety of his makeshift throne. He and Katy aren't the only Narrows kids here, but they are the worst. There's a reason there's open space around their table even though Wonderland is packed. Lucas Attenborough and Katy Smith repulse Legacies so much that no one wants to be anywhere near them, not even if it would mean being able to sit down and watch the room.

I'm scanning for James and Ursula when Dally Star, illustrious owner of this little corner of paradise, summons me over. I push through the crowd and signal to Dally's right-hand man, Gary, to get me a drink. He doesn't ask me what. I always get the Caterpillar, a mix of bitters and tonic water. Even if Wonderland served alcohol and I were old enough to drink in earnest, I wouldn't. I learned early on that it's best to stay sharp at all times.

"Hi, sweetheart." Dally slides my drink to me and I hand over my three dollars. "No, no, don't be silly. It's on the house." Dally's in a white suit, just like he always is, with his thin moustache and white towel slung over his shoulder, blond hair coiffed into a semi-bouffant, white sunglasses with pink lenses. He's probably not more than twenty-five, but he could also be sixty. Dally Star is mercurial and impossible to pin down: in age, in look, in personality. He is an anomaly. But he's also my friend. Sort of.

"Thanks, Dally." I sip on the drink, savour the faint traces of orange in the bitters.

"You want me to hold that for you?" He indicates my backpack, which is now stuffed with work clothes, boots and my coat.

I'm in my usual black jeans and white tank, my leather necklaces on, leather bracelets climbing my arms. I feel like myself again. "Yes, please," I say, handing it to him.

I catch sight of Ursula down by the stage dancing, head leaned back. Ursula dancing is the best. She does it like she does everything else, with total commitment, limbs flailing so she looks like she has more than four, eyes closed like there's no one around her and nothing to pay attention to. People move out of her way so they don't get hit. She'll never even notice.

James is in the corner playing pool where I can just see him from my place at the bar. At first, I want to run over to him and tell him my news, but as usual, watching James leaves me too breathless to do much of anything. I love the way his hair flops from behind his ears so his eyes are hidden from my view, the way his cheeks dip into dimples when he laughs at something. But the biggest thrill I get from James is the aura of danger that's always around him, an invisible bubble. No matter how he smiles, no matter the warmth in his voice, James Bartholomew is always up to something.

If I watch carefully, I'll see that what looks like an innocent game of pool is actually so much more. By dominating the game as he is, surrounded by his boys, he's sending a message to his opponent and his opponent's boys. If I look carefully, I will see that there's money on the table, and James will be lining his pockets with it soon enough, because James never loses. It is a sickness to admit his power has always and will always be the thing that draws me to him the most. That, and knowing I'm the only thing in the world he really cares about.

"So, what's going on with the body parts all over town?" Dally swings the rabbit foot he always carries in his pocket.

I shouldn't be as surprised as I am that Dally knows about that. He knows about everything, has ears to the ground at all times.

"Can't talk about that, Dally."

He is completely unaffected by my denial. "Everyone saw the box that was left in front of the Ever Garden. I heard it was little Chipper Lowry who found it, poor thing. Imagine, three years old! His mother is going to have to explain how a foot came to be in a box at the park gates. Apparently" – Dally leans forward – "Chipper thought it was a toy. Tried to play with it. Howled when his mother took it from him." He sighs. "Oh, to have been a fly on an Ever rose that day."

I smile conspiratorially. "Yes. To have been a fly on an Ever rose."

"Don't listen to the people who say you're betraying the Scar by working for the government, sweetheart," Dally says. "Put them out of your head. They're just jealous."

Dally does this a lot. Pushes buttons and waits for reactions. It's how he gets so much of his information. In spite of best efforts not to let myself get rattled, this does rattle me. The Scar means too much for me to tolerate being seen as a traitor when I'm trying to be the opposite. "People are saying that?"

"Never you mind. Let us be proud of you. You deserve it. You could be at home worrying about your social media, but instead you're contributing to your community, and the Great Ghost knows we need it."

"Dally," I say.

He pours me another drink, eyes on the band. "Mmmm?"

"I was just wondering if you know anything about Mally Saint."

Dally perks up and leans forward, one eyebrow raised. "I heard she's missing. Her father came in here yesterday with that awful bird and some big security guy, looking for her. I don't know a thing, hon. She was here Monday. I saw her acting creepy and bitchy as usual, and then she was gone. As far as I'm concerned, everything was the same as usual. I already showed him the camera footage, but I can show it to you, too, if you want." A look of understanding passes over his face. "Hang on a second," he says. "Are you on an official case?"

I can't help but smile a little.

"Shouldn't you show me your badge, then? Let me know this is official questioning?"

I don't want to admit that all I have is a temporary badge and a can of pepper spray.

"This is wonderful, Mary," he says. "I couldn't be more excited for you. And you'll find her, I have no doubt." He leans on his elbows. "That girl has more enemies than just about anyone in the Scar I can think of. You have plenty of people to talk to, that's for sure. I wish I could help you, be part of your first victory, but alas, I am but a poor little bartender."

I had been half hoping I would walk in here and Dally would solve the case for me and I'd be on my way to glory and fame walking out the door tonight, but I don't let my disappointment show. "Was she with anyone?"

"From what I can remember she left here alone. She's always alone, you know."

"But I've seen her dancing."

"Yeah, she dances alone, always alone. It's sad, really. Dangerous way to live, if you ask me. Safety in numbers and all that."

I let everything Dally said sink in. Somewhere between here and her father's apartment, something happened that disappeared Mally right off the streets. I try to think through it. She lives in the same building as Ursula, about six blocks from here, and there are four blocks of busy businesses and bright lights before it turns into the warehouse district and things get a lot darker. Maybe someone sneaked up on her there.

One thing's for sure. Ursula isn't walking home alone tonight.

Like she heard me, Urs comes running out of the crowd, sweaty and smiling, her blonde hair sticky against her cheeks, bosoms practically bursting from the front of her tight black dress. "Finally!" She pulls on my arm. "Come on, let's go dance!"

"Don't dance. Stay here with me."

Ursula rolls her eyes but smiles and takes my drink. Arms wrap around my waist. I lean back against James and it's like my whole body relaxes for the first time since school. He squeezes me in closer and I spin round on my stool and kiss him.

James and I met after my family died, when I moved onto my block to live with Gia. His father was in prison and his mother had moved to Michigan to get away from everything. She had promised to come back for James, and for a few years we lived in a state of terror, imagining her returning to steal him away. He wanted to see her. He may have even wanted to live with her. But James is a part of the Scar and the Scar is part of him, and the idea of living outside of it was far worse than that of living without his mother. She did finally come back once to visit, but she and James didn't have much to say to each other. By then he had been living with his aunt Della for years.

And then, one day when we were thirteen, while we were staring up at the clear blue sky from the fire escape at my apartment, he said, "I don't think you're just my friend."

I had been contemplating the way the clouds in the Scar change shapes differently than in other places, how when I thought a cloud looked like an elephant, it began marching across the sky, trunk held in a high salute. Clouds hadn't done that when I'd gone to Midcity to pay taxes with Gia. I turned to him questioningly. "You don't think we're friends?"

This was an impossibility. We did everything together. I couldn't remember the last time I'd eaten dinner without James. I was either at his house or the Layer Cake, or we were at my apartment.

"I didn't say that. I said I don't think you're *just* my friend. I said" – he rolled onto his side, rested his head into a hand and stroked my cheek like it was something precious – "that you're going to be my everything. For this lifetime, it's going to be me and you against the world."

What I remember most after that is that the clouds overhead blossomed into flowers with heart-shaped petals. I also remember feeling like something was being repaired, something shredded was stitching itself back together, ragged but no longer open to the world. And then I remember the terror that followed knowing that now I had something I didn't ever want to lose. Even then I had lived long enough to know nothing is really safe.

"You guys are nauseating," Ursula says now. She bounces on her heels to the beat of the music and sends out half a dozen chats, then snaps a picture of herself smiling around a slice of lime. "Truly." She pulls the lime from her mouth with a suctioned slurp. "Get in a fight once in a while."

"Why would we do that?" James says.

"James the Loyal," Ursula says, adjusting her cleavage and pulling at her skirt. "James the Magnanimous. Good thing you've got some mischief in there. Otherwise you'd be too boring to hang out with."

"Aw, Urs. It's nice to know I have your vote of confidence. Makes me feel so much better about my life."

Dally slides a couple of raven wings, a mix of cola and grenadine, their way, and James hands over some of the money he just took off those other guys playing pool. I hold on to his sleeve, one finger inside the cuff, like I've been doing since we started dating. He slides himself behind me so we're both facing Ursula.

"So what happened today in the great grand land of the peacekeepers?" Ursula says.

"Well, *actually*, something did happen."

"Tell! Tell!"

"I got a case."

"What?" James pulls back so he can see me.

"Yeah." I don't know why I'm suddenly shy about it. "It's Mally Saint. She disappeared."

"Oh, she's pushing daisies for sure," Ursula says without missing a beat. "Sort of sad. I was beginning to think we might be friends someday."

"Urs!"

"Well, she's been just awful to everyone. There are people who would like to see me go down, too. But I give them reasons not to try to retaliate in any way. A girl's got to protect herself, and I don't think Mally has those kinds of smarts. She has no self-restraint."

"Yeah, well, the point is she vanished and hopefully is not pushing daisies. And if she's not, I'm going to find her. You shouldn't talk about her like that."

"Oh, come on," Ursula says, "why do you care?"

"I don't know… because she's a person?" Even to them I can't admit the truth. I want Mally to come home alive and well to satisfy my own ambitions.

"Your first real case," James says. "You're going to do great. You're going to find her."

"We'll help!" Ursula says.

"We'll help if you want us to," James says, giving her a look.

"Yeah, I'm hoping you guys will just tell me if you hear anything on the streets, since, you know…" I say.

"People won't talk to you because they think you're betraying the Scar?" Urs says, as if they might be right.

This is the second time this has been mentioned tonight. I got a little bit of a hard time when I first got the internship, but it seems like that's mostly burned off. And yet, maybe it hasn't. I can't think of anything to do to change anyone's mind other than proving to them my goal in working for the government is to help fix it, to fix the Scar and return it to its former glory.

James says, "You find Mally and bring her back, people will start to trust you're on our side. Even though no one likes her, she's still one of us."

"Oh, man, people suck," Ursula says, raising her glass. "But not you guys!"

"But not you!" James and I agree, and we clink our glasses together.

"What do you think?" she says. "Want to go play some croquet?"

"Yes." I slip off my stool. "Gotta keep my name on top of the list."

"You're always on top of my list," James says.

"Actual vomit in my mouth," Ursula says, pulling at the top of her dress, hoops swaying in her earlobes. "I don't know why I hang out with you."

They laugh and keep insulting each other, but I can't keep the feeling I have at bay: that a storm has been brewing under our feet, one I can't even see from here, and that this is the last moment we will all have together before it reveals itself to us. I want to tell them. I want to hold all of us in this moment, safe and sound. I want to put all of us in an impenetrable bubble and float us away from here. But I can't because magic is dead and wishes don't come true anymore.

So I sling my arms around my boyfriend and my best friend and we play croquet in the dark and then we dance hard enough to make the roof come down, because there is nothing else to be done.

SIX

NO MATTER HOW MUCH PEOPLE WANT TO DENY that magic is or ever was, Legacies know Monarch isn't like other places. Traces, like tremors, are all around us, reminding us that we don't know everything and that some things can't be explained. There's the weather, the clouds, Miracle Lake and the black hearts resting like seeds waiting to be fed so they can blossom. People have Traces of magical abilities that are supposed to have been dead for eleven years now, like the way James knows if I'm in a room or if I'm sad or in danger, or the way my dreams sometimes feel like they're telling me something. And then there's also this inexplicable place, where we've always come to hide. It's the best of anywhere, my favourite breadcrumb trail of fairy dust in all of the Scar.

The Ever Garden.

They say the reason the Ever Garden remained is that so much good happened here and so many wishes came true that even after the Great Death it stayed as it had once been. The park spans an entire block right in the middle of the Scar, and is covered from stem to stern in luscious flowers, trees and bushes that can't be found anywhere else. Humans only have three colour cones and can only see dimly compared to butterflies and hummingbirds, but when you set foot in the Ever Garden it feels like the veil has been lifted from your eyes and suddenly you can see everything as it really is. Colours here can only be perceived within its gilded gates. Lilacs shimmer with opalescence. Dahlias drip from porticos in the most exotic persimmon and dragonfruit colours, glittering and diamond like. Black roses, shiny as oil slicks, blast rainbows from one to the other. A brook runs through its centre, crystalline silvery water with votive lotuses floating on top.

But the best part of the Ever Garden is that its infinite nooks and crannies bend to hide its visitors, so if you cross the threshold into the Ever Garden, you will always be alone with the people you came with. There will always be a perfect patch of green grass to lie on for a picnic or to watch the stars overhead. Nothing bad has ever happened in the garden. If anyone even tries, the garden comes alive and ejects the offender. That includes anyone stupid enough to try to prune its branches or change its landscape. Once someone tried to sell hot dogs from a cart and was hurled out by a redwood. It is the one place in the Scar and maybe in the world where nothing bad can happen and nothing is allowed to change.

So this is where James and I come sometimes to be quiet and alone. Unlike the rest of Monarch, this place is slow and safe.

We duck behind a patch of marigolds, and two weeping willows drape their branches around us. We settle onto the grass, the earth warm as a blanket beneath us.

"James?"

"Yeah?"

"Do you think Mally is dead?"

"You really know how to make a date sexy and special and not at all homicidal," he says.

"I'm sorry."

"Don't be. It's important. You might save someone."

"Not if she's already in a dumpster somewhere."

"No." He settles onto his back and pulls me in close, so his heartbeat taps steadily against my ear. "I don't think so."

I'm relieved to hear it. Even though it's only his intuition, his is extra-good. It's what makes him near untouchable. He knows when someone is betraying him and he knows when someone is loyal. He also knows when someone is a lost cause.

"I don't think she's dead, either," I say. "But I've been thinking she might have just left town. Her life is a mess. She is angry, shunned and spiteful. She has nothing but her father's money and her bird. Maybe she decided to leave it all behind and went to reinvent herself somewhere where she's not completely despised."

James seems to think. "No. Mally would never leave that bird. Never. She might leave her father and his money, she might even leave the Scar, but she wouldn't leave Hellion behind."

"How do you know?" I prop myself onto my elbow and stroke his hair back from his brow.

"Because she loves him and he loves her, and she got him right after her mother died, and that's how people work, especially here. We're tied to arbitrary people and things we've been assigned to by fate. That bird is her familiar and she wouldn't go anywhere without him by choice."

"Which means…"

"Which means she's probably somewhere against her will or maybe hurt somewhere. But I don't think she's dead."

"Why not?"

"Because people are like maps. They have lines on them just like the ones in the palms of their hands," he says. "Those lines tell stories and that's not how her story is going to end. You only have to look at her to know it. Mally Saint doesn't just die. That's not her fate. Mally Saint goes out in a blaze of rage." He takes my hand from where it was resting on his chest and holds it up so it's under the light of two glowing bushes, examining it.

"Why are you reading my palm? You already know my lines."

"Just making sure they haven't changed."

"And how do they look?"

"The same."

"And how does our story end?"

He hesitates, his face darkening for a moment before he casts his doubt aside and grins.

"Happily ever after, of course."

He's not exactly lying. I'm sure he wants a happy ending for us both, but things are so jagged and unpredictable in the Scar, he can't really believe everything will be peaches and cream from here on out. That's not the way it works. Not for anyone.

He presses his thumb into the centre of my palm and I close my eyelids and let everything drift away: Mally, Hellion, the chief, Bella, Gia, all my worries, the infighting in Monarch, everything I can't explain, and even my family. I fade into the drumbeat of

James's heart, and for several minutes it's the only thing that matters.

"I just want…" I say. I can't find any more words, but the feeling inside is like flint and rock waiting for enough of a spark to ignite in earnest.

"I know," he says. "You want. I want, too. And someday we aren't going to want anymore because we're going to *have*. I'm making sure of that, Mary." He doesn't move, but after some silence he says, "It feels like something is happening, doesn't it?"

"What do you mean?"

"I don't know. It seems like there are forces at work. The Fall, Miracle Lake, you getting the internship, Mally going missing. It's like we got on a ride no one told us about, and we're strapped in and going to have to stay aboard to see where we end up."

A sprig of mistletoe dangles overhead and covers us in a fine mist of something that smells like Christmas and warm fires. It's true that in the rest of Monarch Christmas is coming, the weather getting colder and harsher. I pull myself up the length of his body and we kiss.

He runs his fingers up the back of my hand, over my ring finger. "Do you remember our first dance?"

"Eighth grade."

"You came rushing down your apartment stairs to meet me."

"Smee went with Ursula. They fought the whole time."

"But you," he says. "You came down in a cloud of gold, your hair even brighter than usual. You had that necklace."

"My mother's pearl choker—"

"And you were beautiful." I kiss him until he laughs. "Don't try to distract me. I'm trying to tell a very important and touching story."

"Oh, fine," I say, "go ahead. But make sure you say more stuff about me being beautiful and perfect. Don't leave out any of the details."

"Well," he says, pulling me in close again, "when you came down those stairs I looked at you and I didn't just see this beautiful girl who was legit going to a dance with me, James Bartholomew. I saw someone who had already stuck by me. You didn't listen to them when they told you I was trash or bad news or never going to amount to anything. You didn't listen to anyone, ever."

"That's the night I gave you this." I kiss his wrist, just above where he still wears the alligator-skin watch.

"You stole it for me from your grandfather's box. Gia tried to take it back the next day."

"I wouldn't let her. You deserved something fine. She said the watch was a family heirloom and I said—"

"You said I *was* family. You made me feel like somebody," he says. "You have always been the only one who didn't see me as someone I'm not. You don't ask me to be any better than I am and you don't think I'm any worse. You know everything about me. Someday," he says, slipping two fingers over my knuckle, "even if it's a long time from now, I hope you'll marry me."

I'm not shocked at the idea of marrying James. This is something I've always assumed. James and I will never find better than each other and we would never want to. Since the day we kissed on that rooftop, I've known he would be my partner in life. If that means being a wife to his husband, I would do that. I wouldn't hesitate. But it isn't something we talk about. We're only seventeen, so I know it's not relevant right now, but it will be, and it feels good to have at least one piece of my life approaching certainty. I'm going to have to fight for everything else.

He pushes himself onto his knees, and I sit up. "Mary Elizabeth," he says. "I know we're not ready yet, but if the world should finally stop shuddering and decide to dim its light once and for all, I would want to be with you. When those buildings fell, before Miracle Lake came, all I could think was how lucky I was to be watching the end of the world with you. When we do marry it's not going to be a prison," he says. "You won't wish you're somewhere else and you won't feel like you want to escape me. We'll both get to do everything we want, because we'll be together and that will make everything possible. Life will be the greatest adventure."

"I don't understand why this is coming up now." Did he do something illegal? Is he in danger? Something about this doesn't feel right.

It's not like we haven't had this conversation before, or some version of it, but he seems even more intense than usual. "Is anything the mat—"

"I won't leave you ever," he cuts me off. "And I need you to promise you won't leave me." He buries his lips against my neck and I arc towards him in spite of my misgivings. His lips are too much of a distraction.

"If I promise you," I say, struggling to keep hold of my thoughts. "Will you tell me the secret?"

"Promise," he insists.

"James." I'm frightened now, all the safety of the Ever Garden burned off. "We're supposed to trust each other. We should be able to tell each other anything. So what is it?"

"I have always supported you," he says.

"I know."

"Even though your internship puts me in a bad place on the streets, and even though it might put us at odds if I end up in the same spot as my dad."

"You won't."

"I might." His face darkens under the moonlight as irises lean towards us to comfort him. "We don't know what's coming for the Scar next and we don't know who will be in power. If it's not the Scar on the winning side, who knows what could happen? You know I'm not going to let the Narrows bully the Scar." He sits across from me. "Well, what if I've found a way to take precautions?"

This, this right here is what I was feeling brewing. This is what's been running under the surface between us. I know it.

"Precautions? Against what?"

"Against weakness," he says. He looks at me searchingly for a reaction, but I don't know what he's saying. "What if I could show you something better than running this town from Midcity, being a cop?"

"James." The word slides off my tongue, a request. I want him to stop as much as I want him to show me, to tell me everything. "I *want* to be a cop. I *want* to run Midcity."

"I'm going to make all our dreams come true, Mary Elizabeth," he says, like he hasn't heard my words. "Do you believe me?"

I don't answer as he opens his palm and lays it flat, then raises it up between us. My skin starts to sing, my Legacy mark throbbing like a pulse.

A blue light curls upwards from his hand, between our chests, which are both rising and falling to the beat of a flapping wing as though we might take flight. We nearly stop breathing as the ball of light hangs in the space between us. James looks unearthly, alien, and brighter and happier than I've ever seen him.

And then I'm remembering the shock of blue light during the Fall, the tearing at my head, reaching up from the centre of the earth like lightning travelling backwards, like angry veins. This looks similar, but is softer, friendlier. It doesn't hurt and it isn't separate from me. It's like a beckoning friend. It's a part of me, even as it hovers, and it's warm, exciting, and has a spirit all its own that it's sharing with us.

"Where did you get it?" I ask him.

"I can't tell you."

"I thought we don't keep secrets from each other."

"Soon," he says. "Trust me."

"Trust," I say.

Trust, a whisper echoes. *Trust us.*

"But, James," I say as the ball of blue light dances around us. "It's…"

"Magic." He is staring at the blue light with the kind of focus he usually reserves for me.

"Yeah," I say.

There is a soft and tingly whir as the light morphs itself into tendrils, spreading to the size of a small watermelon, and the light around it is getting bluer, brighter.

"It wants you to take it," James says.

Sometimes I don't see bad things coming around the corner. I didn't know the Fall was coming. That one took me totally by surprise. Sometimes I don't see the good things, either, and they can be just as surprising as the bad. Like, I couldn't have guessed after my family died that James and I would meet each other and fill in all our broken places. Life is always happening, sometimes too fast to catch. But right now, looking at this blue light in front of me, my stomach flipping all around like an eel in a waterless bowl, I can see this blue light is the beginning and the end of everything. And I know I should ask James about it. I should force him to tell me where he got it, what it is and what it means, but I don't want to because I have a feeling it's going to be an answer I don't want, something that will demand further action. And the thing is, James and I trust each other enough to make mistakes. We trust each other so much we don't have to tell each other everything. There's freedom in that, and it's freedom I don't want to lose.

So I keep looking at this light until I'm a part of it, until I am the swirl and I can see it isn't just a flat blue. It's got little tendrils of purple and green and threads of gold at its centre. It's alive and beckoning, its fingers reaching for me. Half a second later, the light shoots into my chest.

James, I whisper, and just like that I know it's the end of whatever came before it.

This, right now, is the beginning.

James takes hold of me and every memory we've ever shared flashes through my mind and between us.

He's throwing an arm around me for the first time.

He's telling me about his father.

I'm telling him about what happened to my family.

We are trying so hard not to touch, the space between us, electric. I always know where he is in the room and he always knows where I am, too, like every atom that occupies the space between us knows we should always be touching.

And then we are. Our first kiss nearly ends the world.

This doesn't make either of us run away.

We run towards each other instead.

This is trust, the blue light says. *Open.*

We do. I open. When James and I kiss again, lips that have touched thousands of times, it's as though we have millions of new nerves, as though we understand each other, can predict the other's movement, until it feels like we don't have bodies at all and we are nothing but all this light.

All the flowers brighten around us in an iridescent cascade of colour. They sway, dancing for us.

"Mary," James manages, his voice hoarse and ragged. "This is perfect. You are perfect."

This is what the truth feels like.

It feels like love.

SEVEN

MALLY SAINT IS IN MY BED. HER MOUTH MOVES around the letters of my name. Her skin is tinged green, yellow lizard eyes covered in a milky film, and she is being consumed by flames. She's crawling closer. She'll burn my bed. She'll burn everything. If she comes closer we'll both die.

But she does come closer and we don't die. My temperature only rises a little. Mally edges in so her breath is hot on my cheeks. Flames all around her lick at me.

"They're going to take everything for themselves and there will be nothing left of you," she says. "There will be nothing left of anyone."

She pushes through my skin, each layer of muscle and then bone parting to make way for her burning pointer finger. Something comes loose inside me. When she pulls her arm back, she is holding a thumping lump in her hand, and blood drips down her arm in black rivulets.

I clutch at my chest, trying to close the gaping hole, looking around for something to stop the wound.

"Mary Elizabeth," she says, holding my heart in her hand. "You're going to have to decide between your head and your heart. We all do."

My breath is slipping away and I take her by the wrists. This is what it is to die. There is so much unfinished, so much I'll never do. I want to call for James, for Ursula, but I don't have the strength to make a sound. The closer she gets, the more I struggle to breathe. Her perfume is sweet with decay.

"Are you dead?" I ask her, but I don't think I use my voice when I do.

She places a finger on her chin and looks upwards as though the answer is in the ceiling. Then she brings her face close to mine.

"I miss my bird." She cocks her head to the side. "Have you seen Hellion, Mary Elizabeth?

"Mary Elizabeth, do you hear me?

"Do you hear?

"Mary Elizabeth?

"*Mary Elizabeth?*

"Mary Elizabeth! Wake up."

I open my eyes to a blinding light that is white and harsh, and a pounding headache, and for a second I think I've been kidnapped and am about to be questioned under a single light bulb. Then I realise I'm in my room and the backlit creature responsible for the torture is Bella. Who is in my house.

I reach for the bedside table, run my fingers past the half-filled glass of water and the book on forensics I've been trying to read, and I try to bring the screen on my phone into focus.

"Six thirty? What the hell?" I don't even know what time I got home last night… this morning. Probably a couple of hours ago at most. The light. James.

"Good morning, sunshine," Bella says. "Welcome back to the Scar. It's another beautiful day. Not a cloud in the sky."

"Bella, how did you even find my house?"

"Elementary, my dear."

I squint up at her, phone in hand, trying to unblur my room. She sighs. "I got it from the database."

"Invasion of privacy."

"Your aunt let me in. She's still awake."

There are texts from James all across my screen.

I love you.

Then: *I have to do something today. I'll see you after.*

Then: *Have a magical day,* with three laughing emojis and a couple of wands.

The smell of Mally Saint still cloys, so waves of nausea roll over me, and I feel my chest, then sink back against the pillow when I find I'm not an open wound; not missing a heart and not filled up with blue light, either. Just regular me: achy, disgruntled, possibly haunted.

Bella, on the other hand, is a ray of sunshine.

"Wow," she says, flinging the blinds all the way open. "This is some view. Do you realise how lucky you are? You look right out onto Miracle Lake. I can't see anything from my window except the people next door, and trust me when I tell you that's not anything you would want to see."

"Shut the blinds, monstrous human!"

Bella totally ignores me. It's like I'm not even talking. She's too busy at the window, gawping at Miracle Lake in an adorable outfit of a T-shirt and high-waisted trousers held up by suspenders. Her makeup is flawlessly neutral and her hair is in a sloppy bun. I bet it took her an hour to get dressed and here she is, crisp and delightful in my bedroom and it's not even seven a.m.

"Were you in here during the Fall? It must have been right outside your window." She's all curiosity and enthusiasm. I must have done something very bad to deserve this fate. "Did you see it?" she says.

"I saw," I say, and then have to shake off the memory. "Bella, again I ask you. What are you doing in my apartment?"

"Well." She seems to be thinking. "We're partners. We have a case. You have not responded to any of my texts. Hence and therefore I had no choice but to come to you. And according to your file, you are free most of the day, which is excellent news because we've got no time to waste. We need to find Mally, preferably today, so come on! Let's get going!"

"Right," I say. "But I thought we were going to meet after school. *At the station.*"

"Yes, however…" She bounces onto my bed and crosses her legs in front of her. "I'm going to see if I can speak to those three girls while you're in your math class. Which reminds me…" She goes into her leather satchel and pulls out some papers. "I did your math homework. That way you don't have to worry about it and we can really focus."

"You did my…"

"I'm a whiz on the computer, you know. I found it with the school portal. This math is a breeze. It was no problem."

"Thank you?"

"Well?" She gives me an expectant smile. "I don't know about you, but I'm pretty sure having been missing for three days means Mally isn't going to find herself, and every minute counts."

"I want to interview Flora, Fauna and Merryweather with you."

Bella shakes her head. "I don't think that's a good idea. You're a peer. With me they won't have any preconceptions.

"I already checked and Mally hasn't used her credit cards anywhere," Bella goes on. "Not even her city transport card. Obviously she hasn't showed up anywhere she's supposed to be, nor is she visiting relatives out of town. So I guess what I'm saying is considering a life hangs in the balance, we should get cracking! We need to discuss all the possibilities and our strategy. And then of course if she's deceased—"

"She's alive."

Bella's nose twitches slightly as she stops her rant long enough to look my way. "I never said she wasn't, but we have to consider it's a possibility. We both know how the numbers work after the first forty-eight hours, and they aren't in our favour."

"I had a dream," I say.

"Dream?"

"Yes, I had a dream about Mally. Dreams are my Trace. So she's alive and I know it because she told me."

"Huh." Bella plops down beside me. "So you're a Magicalist?"

I'm taken aback by the audacity of her question and the plain way she asked it. There isn't anything more personal than asking a Legacy her views on magic, and any association cuts close to the bone. Magicalists are extremists, Amagicalists are amoral magic deniers, also extremist, and Naturalists are seen as befuddled, ridiculous and irrelevant middle-aged housewives. Any way you look at it, assuming an affiliation is something you just don't do. But here she is, open-faced and innocent, asking me the most personal of questions.

"I don't like labels," I snap. "And I think the Magicalist methods are a little obvious." They riot, cause public mischief, undermine the city because they think the city council is hiding magic from the rest of us, that they were somehow responsible for the Great Death. "What about you?" If we're going to have this conversation, it's going to be tit for tat.

She shrugs. "I don't know. I believe what I see. I don't see any point in being an Amagicalist. We know it was here once. It does seem like a little bit of a joke that all we get as a reminder of what we once were is West Coast weather and suggestion-responsive cumulus clouds."

But that's not true, is it? We also have whatever it is that James was wielding last night. I think of the blue light, the whirring, the feeling like I was finally alive. I can understand why people who had experienced it once would want it again and again, especially if they felt it was their birthright. It makes sense that the Magicalists are so upset. "Well, whether you believe in Traces or not, I had one last night. It doesn't happen often, but sometimes I get a dream that isn't really a dream, and even if most of it doesn't make sense, there's always a kernel of something to pay attention to."

"Okay, I'll bite. Supposing your dream was real or sending you a message of some kind. Did she tell you anything else?" Bella has one eyebrow raised in what I'm beginning to recognise as her most active facial expression. So far I've seen it mean she's being naughty, confusing or saying something she doesn't quite believe. "Anything?"

"No." I hear the sickening sound of my heart being dislodged and have to bring myself back to my room so I don't go into a panic. "She told me she misses her bird."

You're going to have to choose between your head and your heart, Mary Elizabeth. I shudder.

"Well, that doesn't seem like a very useful dream, does it?"

"You know what, Bella? You can just—"

Bella lays her head on the pillow next to mine like we're at a sleepover. It's like she has no boundaries at all whatsoever. "Anything else, then? Ideas?"

I watch her profile and consider how easy it would be to smother her. Other than that, I'm not sure there's a cure for her delirious optimism. I sigh and give in. After all, we're in this together whether I like it or not. I'll learn to withstand the twinkle in her eye eventually.

With effort.

"I talked to Dally Star last night," I say. "You know, the owner of Wonderland?"

"I know who he is. Can't say I've ever been in Wonderland before. Not really my thing."

I try to imagine Bella thrashing to alt rock on a Friday night or playing pinball croquet, and come up absolutely empty. "No, I bet it's not."

"So what did he say?"

"He told me Mally left Wonderland alone last week."

"Well, let's get that camera footage and prove it, then."

"Yes, I was going to ask—"

"I'll do it today!" she says, bouncing off the bed. "Well, come on!"

The smell of the coffee Gia always makes in the morning drifts into my room. I slip a black T-shirt over my head, and Bella looks away, reddening. I grab my badge and tuck it where it can't be seen, and slide into some jeans, then drag on my boots as my alarm goes off. I guess it's not so bad. I would be waking up at this time anyway, and actually, today is the first day I really feel like a cop. Yes, I'll have to get through stupid math and stupid history, but then I'll have my first afternoon as a real, actual detective on a real, actual case.

At Bella's eyeline is a picture of me, my parents and Mirana visiting what was once the enchanted forest.

"Your family?" she says.

"Yes. They were."

She doesn't say anything but nods. Almost everyone in the Scar has lost someone close to them. Best not to remark on it every single time. We've all learned to live with it.

As I get my jacket and scarf from the wardrobe, Bella's eyes skate all over my room, taking in its details, recording everything. A Legacy flag with a black heart is tacked to the wall above my bed, which is covered in black sheets and a black duvet. Other than that and a couple of pictures of my family, there is only a map of the Scar and the larger, framed picture of me with the chief and Mayor Triton at the press conference when I was seven. My clothes, of which I don't have many, are hung neatly in a small wardrobe, and my jewellery is stacked in a bowl on my dressing table. A distressed mirror that my mother acquired during the magic-mirror days returns a slightly distorted reflection, and a black shag rug covers the floor. Next to the door, five pairs of black boots are lined up, each a different size and in a different state of wear.

"I'll give you a minute," Bella says as I gather my things.

Even though the Scar is full of skaters and the roads are littered with shirtless loiterers in flip-flops, I stick to the same uniform, one that allows me to adjust to the weather no matter where I am in Monarch and to leave my apartment quickly no matter the situation: a T-shirt, black jeans, boots and the layered choker I always wear at my neck, with five dangling silver hearts that fall at my throat. I slip on my leather bracelets, then grab my backpack and stuff my jacket and umbrella inside, and then text James to tell him not to come get me this morning. I'm not ready to explain Bella to him just yet, and I don't even know what would happen if Bella had to ride to school with Smee and Ursula.

"I met your partner," Gia says when I emerge from the bedroom. She's in her orange-and-red pyjamas, getting ready for bed, hair in two loose plaits.

"How nice," I drawl, presenting my cup to be filled. As soon as it is, I take a sip of the bitter liquid.

"Coffee, sweetie?" she says, pouring some into a cup for Bella, who finds cream and sugar and a small spoon. Gia lets out a loud yawn. "Sorry. It was quite a night on the other side of the planet. And you," she says to me. "We might have to reinstate a curfew if you're going to come in so late."

I don't remember anything about coming home, but I'm afraid to ask her any questions. If she knows I don't remember anything, that'll set off so many alarm bells I'll never be allowed to leave the house again. "James and I lost track of time. We were at the Ever Garden."

Gia nods and takes a seat at the small wooden kitchen table.

"At least you were somewhere safe."

She's relaxed about James over time, since she's figured out he's not a bad person like his dad, and that his primary objective is to see that I'm safe at all times. But as soon as she finds out about Mally's disappearance, her paranoia is going to be in full effect. Losing a twin sister to murder will do that to a person.

Bella takes a sip of coffee, then smells it appreciatively. "This is delicious. Thank you."

"You're welcome, dear." She turns to me. "And you. Remember you have math homework and we have an agreement. School first!"

Bella winks from behind Gia and I have to stifle a groan.

"And there's a meeting tonight," she tells Bella proudly. "Naturalists."

"Ah," Bella says.

"Anyway, we'll be up to our incantations and whatnot, so you just go on into your room if you don't want to join the circle."

I cast a glance at Bella, who looks amused.

"Yes, ma'am. What would I do without you, G?" I know what I would do. Probably perish on a corner like those other people. Gia is my family and I love her even though she makes her money selling Scar makeup over the phone to people across the globe, which seems sketchy at best. It's why she's up all night and heads off to bed right as I'm leaving for school each morning.

I pick up a pancake from a plate on the table, fold it in half and shove it in my mouth, while in the other hand I get my portable coffee mug and fill it with another generous helping of sloshing hot black coffee as she has already had one cup of coffee. "Okay, then. Let's get out of here. And you can come to school with me, but once we're through the doors you're on your own. I'll meet you at Mally's this afternoon. Got it?"

Bella puts her hands up. "Sure! I won't even acknowledge your existence."

"Perfect. Please don't."

"It was nice to see you, honey!" Gia calls as Bella makes mute apologetic gestures and the door slams behind us. "And nice to meet you, Bella!"

EIGHT

THE REASON I KNOW THE UNIVERSE PRETTY much hates me is that out of the fifteen hundred or so students that go to Monarch High School, it not only put me in a history class called the History of Magic in Monarch with Lucas and Katy, it went on to put me in a discussion group with them.

It's bad enough the Narrows are multiplying in the Scar, more of them enrolling down here than ever as their parents move into chic, newly-constructed lakeside apartments. You'd think being infiltrated by a bunch of rich, elitist blowhards would be the worst of it, but then they speak and all this rubbish spills out all over everyone. Plus, they're bullies. It's really kind of impressive how lame they are. There are a few of them that are okay, I suppose, but the ones that are tolerable want to be Legacy so badly they try to dress like us, sometimes even get fake Legacy tattoos they hide from their parents. But they aren't Legacy. They're uptown Narrows and they will be Narrows forever.

At least I have Ursula in this class with me and she's positioned her chair against mine in her own group so she can be ready if I need backup in any way. She's in the midst of a business deal, handing some poor unfortunate soul a finished history paper on the sly. She can get anything for anyone, and even though the Narrows drive her as crazy as they do me, she's not above cosying up to them if they'll pay the right price, and they have the most money so it follows she interacts with them more than I do. It also follows that because of this, she commands a certain level of respect from them.

We spend class texting each other under our desks and sending each other memes. Ursula occasionally gifts me footage of something juicy she witnessed. Mr Iago is so in love with the class he teaches that he doesn't notice any of it.

"Class, class, class," he says, clapping his palms together. "Today we're going to be covering the Midcity Riots."

There's a rumble as Legacy kids start side conversations with one another.

"Why does literally everything have to be about magic and your precious powers that no longer exist so who cares?" Katy says, her blonde ponytail swinging like twitchy horsehair.

Lucas Attenborough crosses his arms and leans back. "Hear, hear."

"This class is *actually* called the History of Magic in Monarch. Legacies are the descendants of people with powers. So what do you *want* it to be about?" Ursula is probably the vainest person I've ever met. She's tall, she's big, and she stands when she's feeling serious about something, which is what's happening right now.

"Ursula, may we have your attention?" Mr Iago says.

"Sure you can." She bats her eyelashes at him and sits down.

"Excellent!" He claps again. "As you know, the thirteen-year anniversary of the March on Midcity is coming right up, and people are going to have a lot of opinions about a lot of things. But I'm not interested in their opinions. I'm interested in what *you* have to say. Was it a good choice having that march? Was it effective in changing minds uptown?" Everyone stares at him. No one says anything. I almost feel sorry for the guy. He probably goes home and waters his ficus every night and cries in his pillow because he has to deal with us all day. "Miss Heart?"

Drat. He must have seen me thinking nice things.

"Um…" I look at him, then to Ursula, who shrugs. "It was fine?"

I know some things about the march. I know Aunt Gia went with my mom and dad and Mirana, and I stayed home with Mimi and Grandpa. That was before they got upset enough to move to California. I know Gia thinks it was important and that she's always talking about all the great musicians who were there and that they were trying to get magic back or something. But come to think of it, I don't really know what it was about, partly because I was out with James last night and did not even slightly do my homework, and partly because at this point it's hard to imagine people fighting for anything on the streets. Now everything is quietly hostile underground, and our efforts seem useless.

"I can answer that. It was not fine." Lucas sits up. Getting on his anti-Legacy soapbox is his favourite thing to do. "Legacy demonstrators cost Monarch hundreds of thousands of dollars. Exactly like Legacies would do, they looted and stole and messed everything up. And what did they accomplish? Nothing. Magic is still dead and their stupid conspiracy theories about the government are irrelevant."

"Well…" I can see Iago choosing his words. "I see your point, Lucas, though I would perhaps argue that they did have good intentions and were rightly upset by the treatment of Scar citizens in general after the Great Death. The fact that there was no magic made this whole area somewhat irrelevant, and the government simply let everything fall into disrepair. We were missing some infrastructure. For instance, one couldn't simply vanish one's trash anymore. One needed a garbage person to come and take it away." He pushes his glasses up the bridge of his nose and they immediately slide down again. He's sweating. This is probably a hard topic for him to cover at school as he is Legacy himself. It's so controversial and the school is supposed to be neutral. "They needed to do something to shine a light on what was happening to them, don't you think?

"Legacy acted like trash after the Great Death. They stole and lied. And my mother always says, 'Act like trash, get treated like trash.'" Katy folds her arms across her chest.

"Oh, does she, now?" Ursula looks like she might stand again. "I'm curious, what does your mom do for a living, again?" She taps her chin. "Oh, right. Nothing. She gets her nails done and goes for spa weekends while this neighbourhood perishes because of all the new businesses you guys are bringing in. You're nothing but annoying little ticks."

"Loser," Lucas whispers. "Magic is dead. Get. Over. It."

Ursula smiles. "There are a lot of ways to skin a cat, Lucas." She plucks a hair from his head and deposits it in her cleavage. Lucas blanches. "Careful, or I'll put you on my naughty list."

"Crazy witch," Lucas mutters under his breath, just loud enough for us to hear.

"You make me feel such primal violent urges, Lucas," I say.

He looks at me as though noticing my presence for the first time since class started, even though he's been sitting across from me for the better part of twenty minutes.

"Aren't you a cop?" he says.

"Yeah," Katy echoes. "Like, aren't you supposed to protect civilians?"

"I'm an intern, which means I can do whatever I want." I say that, but it's not true. If I actually did get into a physical altercation, my internship would come to an abrupt end.

"Okay, all right," Iago says. "Mary Elizabeth, Lucas and friends, I would like to remind you that this is a safe space and we will consider all points of view. That is ultimately what we're looking for as we review our rich and complex history. What mistakes have been made, and how can they be avoided in the future, uh, the future of course being now?" He clears his throat. "We can all agree that the March for Magic didn't go as planned; however, the point of it, the original intent, was relevant."

"How?" Lucas says. "How does a bunch of morons stealing TVs help anything?"

"That was after," Ursula says. "After the city started using tear gas. And it was from one of their big stores. It was a political statement. No one wanted that to happen at first. My mom was there. She said it was chaos and people just started freaking out."

Lucas isn't intimidated by Ursula. He doesn't need anything from her and he has more money than anyone anywhere.

"The idea," Mr Iago says, raising his voice over the murmur echoing through the classroom, "and the reason for the march were simple enough. Even after the Great Death, children were being born with the Legacy markings. For the citizens of the Scar, this was monumental. For them, it meant there was some legacy of magic present in their children, and perhaps there was a chance magic could return. The citizens of the Scar had been abandoned, you see, and what was once a thriving community was now reduced to rubble – closed shop fronts. You know the rest. The Legacies were presumed to be there for a reason. For the previous generation, it was the intersection of magic and the Legacy that gave them purpose. And now the Legacies remained; however, their purpose without magic is something of a mystery."

"They just need something to fertilize them," I say, repeating what I've heard so many times from Aunt Gia and the Naturalists. I rest my hand over the black heart Legacy mark on my wrist. The room goes very quiet and I realise I should have kept this thought to myself because now everyone is staring at me like I'm supposed to say something else. "If the Legacy marks are still here, the potential for magic is here, too. They just need like… a spark or something." I think of the blue light.

"That's desperation," Katy says. "If it was true, we would have seen it by now."

"Anyway, the whole thing was probably a hoax," Lucas adds.

"Lucas," I say, "it's your personal choice to be an idiot, but you're insulting people in this room whose families sacrificed a lot in the struggle after magic died."

"Okay, okay," Iago says. "Safe space, safe space. I'm loving the Socratic dialogue, but let's not go overboard."

"I think what Mr Iago is getting at is that your need to engage in confrontations with me boils down to attraction and sexual tension." Lucas stretches his legs a little wider and yawns.

"Uh, no, no. That's not what I was saying," Mr Iago says.

Lucas leans towards me. "And if you didn't have that ugly birthmark and weren't totally concave in the chest area, I might consider relieving all that tension for you."

"That's it!" Ursula gets to her feet. "You and me, jerk. Let's find out how much of a jellyfish you actually are."

"That won't be necessary." The voice that comes from the open doorway is butter and growl, and we all freeze at the impossible figure hovering there. "I'm afraid Lucas is needed elsewhere."

Lucas blanches, face wiped clean of expression.

Ursula backs off and slides her hands on her hips, looking with utter fascination at Kyle Attenborough, Lucas's father and the business mogul behind every new building in Monarch, especially all the glossy new high-rises sprouting up in the Scar. We're all accustomed to being assaulted by his image on billboards and the backs of buses and in train stations, telling all of us about new construction and a multitude of jobs for Scar folk, but to see him in person is something different. He's regal, sure, but he looks… dangerous or something. Also a little shorter than in pictures. Lucas always gets dumped out of a limo on the school front lawn, so Kyle's not much more than a shadow. I've never seen him in person and I'm sorry to say he cuts an impressive figure.

"Oh good," Ursula says, never taking her eyes from his. "Lucas, Daddy's here. Maybe he can teach you some manners."

Kyle wears an unwavering expression of total certainty and

takes a moment too long running his eyes over Ursula's Legacy marking before saying, "Lucas, are you going to introduce me to your friend? You seemed to be in the middle of something."

"Her?" Lucas points to Urs. "Nope. Not worth the introduction."

"Are you sure?"

"Completely sure."

Mr Iago is a mess trying to get to the door, his clothes catching on desks, his feet bumping into their legs. He extends his hand, which Kyle Attenborough considers a beat too long before taking. He's so thin it could almost make a person overlook the physical power he exudes, but I can make out lean muscles under his trouser legs, and his torso is wiry and overdeveloped in the chest and arms.

"Something's come up." Kyle waves a hand in the air. "A family situation. Lucas is needed at home at once."

Mr Iago tilts back on his heels. "Of course you'll need to sign out with the front office."

Kyle Attenborough smiles indulgently. "Certainly," he says. He pulls a card from his inside coat pocket. "And I'm delighted to meet one of Lucas's teachers. Here's the number to my private cell. Please don't hesitate to call me if something comes up with my boy. He can be a little unruly, so I do my best to keep him in line."

"Dad," Lucas says.

Ursula snorts, and Lucas flips her off just out of sight of the adults.

Kyle Attenborough offers a quick half smile to the staring kids and says, "I do apologise for the interruption."

He turns to leave but then pauses on Ursula again. His gaze is unsettling, but she meets it.

"I trust you'll resume smoothly," he says, "and there will be no need for whatever retaliation you were about to deliver to my son, who surely deserved it."

Ursula lifts one side of her mouth into some semblance of a smile.

And then Kyle Attenborough is gone, taking Lucas with him.

"I can't believe Mr Attenborough came to our school," Katy says as soon as the door is closed behind them. "He's so amazing. He's going to bring Monarch back! And I've been to his house lots of times. He even has me over for Christmas."

"That's the idiot who forced my nanna out of her house," Stone says. "We should kick his ass, not kiss it."

"I think he's kind of fascinating," Ursula says. "I mean, who else would have come into the Scar and taken over like that?"

Mr Iago clears his throat and raises one finger to silence us. The classroom goes quiet and everyone stares ahead.

"Well, uh," Mr Iago says, "I think that's enough for today, don't you? For tomorrow the homework is to ask your families where they were during the riots, whether you're Legacy or not. They'll remember."

I don't need to ask. I know. Gia was in the middle of all of it, holding up posters and protesting to anyone who would listen. The Scar should remain the Scar until magic came back and it could take back its true name, Wonder. And in the meantime, after years of doing good and making wishes come true, its citizens deserved some support from the government that had used them and then discarded them.

"Hey, Peace Officer Heart, don't you have to dip so you can go save the world or something?" Urs says.

I glance at my phone. She's right. I do have to go.

"You going to be okay?"

"You know what?" Ursula looks round. "I'm not in the mood for toying with suckers. I've had about enough of this place. Got to go home and check in with Ma." Ursula's mom is always sick, always in bed, and Urs has a little sister she loves who stays home with their mom. The whole thing is not great, and Urs knows it. That's why she says she needs to make a lot of money. She's saving so she can help them and Morgana can go to school, so her mom can get the right health care.

"You have math this afternoon," I remind her.

"Yeah, and?" She shows me her black notepad. "I know how to do math… all the math that matters."

Sometimes Ursula worries me. Like now.

Outside the subway station it's 22°C and sunny, as always. Not quite hot enough for sunbathing, but still one of the things that draws people to the Scar and makes them willing to fight for a place in it. Not a cloud in the sky. The yolky orb of the sun cheerily sending light on our ten-block-by-ten-block square.

"Ugh." Ursula pats her blonde hair and looks upwards. "Can I get a breeze? Falling leaves? Snow? Or even better, make it hot enough I can take a dip in Miracle Lake."

"Ursula," I admonish.

Miracle Lake is deadly. In the first days after the Fall, people didn't know. Even though the water in Miracle Lake is so dark it appears black, and even though it had come to Wonder in the first days after the Fall, people thought maybe it was a blessing. It was only when half a dozen people went in and never resurfaced that the city council and the citizens realised Miracle Lake is a poison so deadly it can't even be tested. Now there are signs posted all over.

As for the weather, it seems best not to think about it too much, and just to be glad that the fact that it hasn't changed in eleven years hasn't completely destroyed the ecosystem. Despite the scientific community's consternation, plants thrive well enough and our water sources don't dry up.

A flyer for an upcoming magic support group is at my feet, trampled several times over.

The first step is admitting you're addicted to magic.

The second step is admitting magic is dead.

Join us! Freedom is nigh.

Amagicalist meeting: Merrypetal Church, Tuesdays at 7:00 p.m.

My aunt Gia hates the Amagicalists, makes the word sound like spit and venom when she speaks it. According to her, to deny magic is to deny life itself. The Naturalist leaders meet at my apartment once a month to discuss ways in which they might be able to raise the vibrations enough to bring magic out of hiding, then they each go to their own sectors and hold simultaneous meetings to try to make something more permanent happen. They believe if enough people set the same intention at the same time, we can bring magic back. They aren't like the Magicalists, who would do anything to bring magic back, at any cost.

"Get your flower crowns," a man calls from the pavement, ribbons blowing across his chest. "Be the princess you always dreamed you'd be." He sounds so unenthusiastic he might as well be selling Q-tips. "Glass slippers, two dollars," he says. "One-day sale only."

We pass by a store front that still reads ENTER TO MAKE A WISH COME TRUE. The letters are faded. Now this store carries milk and a few borderline-rotten fruits and vegetables. The elderly, bent couple that owns the place can always be seen through the window, sitting on stools, wearing sequin robes that were once grand and now seem cheap and garish. They wave to us as we pass.

Ursula bristles. "Someday I'm going to buy them a pony. It's just not right."

"Spare some change?" a man with a staff says. "I lost my house, lost my job, my wife. A few dollars? Anything would help."

He staggers in our direction.

"You can hold it right there, bub," Ursula says, brandishing some pepper spray. "Don't make another move."

"He just wants money, Urs. He's not going to hurt us." I shove a dollar in his hand. Ursula points the pepper spray at him the whole time.

When we get to my apartment building, Gia buzzes us in. As soon as we're in the safety of the courtyard her orange hair flashes like a siren above us, red muumuu flapping out like butterfly wings. "'Morning!" she yells down brightly.

Ursula smiles up at her. "Auntie G, it is not morning."

"Morning to me!" She squints. "I'm just having my tea. Ursula, aren't you supposed to be at school? You're not in the half-day programme, are you?"

"No," Ursula admits, without any shame. "But if I don't chase M.E. around I barely see her now that she's interning."

The window opens on the second floor, and my neighbour, Art, pokes his head out. He looks at us grumpily. "Oh, it's you."

"Hey, Art!" Ursula says. "Looking mighty dapper today."

He checks himself out in his dirty white T-shirt and waves her off. "Compliments are for fools. Would you be quiet and let an old man take a nap?" Art used to be the best landscaper around. When he was young, he could plant a bed of flowers and magic an orchard with a touch of his hands: berries and burdocks, roses and hillocks, grand willow trees and shimmering aspen. Anything a person could dream up he could create, and better than they could have imagined it. Now he mostly sleeps, and sometimes complains, looking dolefully at his useless hands. There's not much else to do.

Mayor Triton was the one who started giving Legacies stipends after the March. To keep the peace. To keep Legacies quiet. After all, the last thing she wanted was another riot. The money is barely enough to survive on, but for people like Art at least it's something.

"Shh." Aunt Gia presses a finger to her lips and motions for us to come up. "Stop being so loud. Art's trying to nap!"

He waves us off and mutters as he disappears back into his apartment and slams the window shut.

We wedge ourselves into the brass-and-glass elevator that takes much longer than if you just walk up yourself. The elevator is as old as this building, which is creeping up on 150 years. No one knew when this place was built that it would one day become lakeside property. It was a four-storey building housing Legacies, shielding them from the constant demands of their clients. Now we have a never-ending stream of people trying to get apartments here, talking about tearing this place down and rebuilding, and hanging out outside by the lake with their beach chairs.

Aunt Gia inherited our apartment from my grandparents,

who died within days of each other before the Great Death. My mother lived here when she was a kid. It was here we would come for holidays, here we would come as a family to celebrate, here I witnessed the Fall. Here is where I came with my suitcase in hand when my parents and sister were murdered.

"Girl, please push that door open," Ursula says. "I need a beverage." She sniffs. "Oh heaven, Gia's baking. Smells like spice cake to me."

As we pass through the entryway into the apartment, I lay my hand across the picture of my dead family, of my mother with her dark, melty eyes and shock of orange hair like Aunt Gia, and my father with his dreamy smile and long lashes. I let my hand linger over my sister, Mirana, with her delicate features, dark hair to match my father's, glancing hopefully at the camera.

It keeps the dead safe to acknowledge them.

Gia emerges from our tiny kitchen with two cups of tea.

"Oooo, tea!" Ursula says, happily, swooping in to give Gia a kiss on the cheek and take the tea from her hands.

"Want some honey?" Gia asks, passing the other cup to me.

"I'll get it," Ursula says, disappearing into the small kitchen. "This is so good, G! Do I smell cake?"

"Ten minutes left to bake!" Gia says.

Ursula comes back in and flops onto the couch, taking an appreciative slurp of her tea.

"What are you doing today?" Gia says. "Guns? Bombs? Running ten miles?"

"No, G. That part's over. Now we're actually on cases. I mean, I just got assigned one, actually."

"I knew they'd let you shine sooner or later," Gia says, beaming.

The old red phone rings from the wall, and since I'm closest I answer.

"Hello."

"Hello." Cindy, Gia's Naturalist friend. "May I speak with Gia?"

"Sure."

Gia is already there to take the phone from me. She knows I don't get calls on this line. "Yes," she begins. "Yes, I have the crystals. Do you have the singing bowls? Great."

I leave Gia to discuss Naturalist plans, and find Ursula is in a heavy sleep on the sofa, her phone dropped on the floor next to her, her teacup emptied beside it. People are afraid of her because she's big and loud and unapologetic about everything she does, and also because she stomps around in black lace-up boots that look like they could do some serious damage, but if they could see her like this, curled up and snoring lightly, I'm sure they'd realise she's just a person. The truth is she's exhausted, working herself to the bone to keep her mother and sister afloat.

I sling a light blanket over her as Gia comes round the corner.

"Bless her heart," she says, then pats me on the back. "You go on."

I clip my temporary badge into place. "You sure?"

"I'll give her some spice cake when she wakes up. We'll be fine." Gia is a kind soul. While I know I've given her plenty to worry about over the years with the boyfriend I have and the people I hang out with, and the many, many calls she's received from the school when I've lost my temper, I never forget that when my family was killed she never hesitated. She took me right in, marched down to the police station, and didn't let me spend one night without a home. She has been there ever since, and in a way she does the same for Ursula, for James, and even sometimes begrudgingly for Smee.

Gia gives me a soft squeeze. "You're going to be late, kid." She points to the clock on the wall.

"I'm going I'm going." I shove my foot into my second boot, stuff my phone and public transportation card into my back pocket, and dash out the door.

I run to the station feeling divided clean in half. Half Scar, half Midcity; half cop, half underbelly; half-hopeful, and half-sure we're all heading for certain doom.

TRANSCRIPT FROM INTERVIEW
TAKEN AT MONARCH HIGH SCHOOL

by Officer Isabella Loyola (Legacy)

Interviewees: Flora (Legacy), Fauna (Legacy), Merryweather (Legacy)

Merryweather: Is this about the demon? Her disappearance?

Officer Loyola: Uh, if you're referring to Mally Saint…

Flora: Yeah, like M said… the demon.

Officer Loyola: I would prefer to refer to her by her name for the purposes of this interview.

Fauna: Would you settle for Mally Saint Demon?

Officer Loyola (clearing throat): When is the last time you saw Mally?

Flora: She was at Wonderland on Monday after school.

Officer Loyola: And you were there as well?

Flora: Yeah, that's where everyone goes after school, like every day. Nothing else to do in the Scar unless you're really into vintage shopping or trolling for vinyl on the strip.

Officer Loyola: And did any of you interact with her at Wonderland?

Merryweather: Oh my ghosts, no. Why would we ever do that?

Officer Loyola: But you were once friends, were you not?

Fauna: I guess you could call it that, but it was like super tox.

Flora: She was so controlling. "Do this, don't do that."

Merryweather: "Change your make up. Your hair is embarrassing."

Flora: Well, you curl your bangs, M.

Merryweather: It's IN STYLE. Read the mags.

Fauna: It was just like we couldn't do anything right. So even though we've known her for like ever, we had enough. Cut her off. Snippety-snip.

Flora: And now we don't have to listen to her go on and on about how her mommy was the fairy queen and our moms are just wannabe losers and we don't have the right look for fairy Legacy. Like, it's not a competition.

Officer Loyola (sighing): So none of you spoke to her on Monday or had any contact with her whatsoever?

Merryweather: Nope. Strict no-hag policy in our crew. And anyway, once someone bleaches your lawn, you kind of keep your distance.

Flora: Yeah, and an actual dead squirrel on your doorstep. That's major trauma. I wouldn't be surprised if someone took her out. Everyone hates her and her stupid bird, too.

Officer Loyola: Well, okay. I hope you'll make

yourselves available if I have any further questions.

Merryweather: We still have a half hour of PE. Can we maybe hang out in here?

Flora: Yeah, you don't want to mess up those bangs!

(sound of snorting laughter)

Officer Loyola: This is Officer Isabella Loyola, and this concludes this interview.

NINE

SINCE WE HAVE TO WAIT FOR THE CAMERA footage from Wonderland to get pulled and processed, and Bella's interview with Flora, Fauna and Merryweather turned up nothing except a rant from Bella about how happy she is to be out of that school and away from teenagers (*no offence, Mary Elizabeth*), Bella and I climb the stairs to Mally's apartment in silence.

Even though Mally isn't here, the building feels cavernous and haunted, silent in a way that's unusual for the Scar. It's in the warehouse district and used to provide all the magical clothes: wizard hats and cloaks, magic wands and those beautiful dresses fairy godmothers gave out when making wishes come true, among so many other things. Now it's pretty much abandoned. I don't even want to know what's inside those empty warehouses. A couple of them make T-shirts now that say things like I SURVIVED THE SCAR and RIP MAGIC. It's also Ursula's block, so I know it pretty well. I've spent plenty of time sitting on Ursula's stoop staring up at the building with the giant iron raven on its roof and sometimes as many as twenty live ravens flying in and out of its top windows.

We're buzzed in immediately by a German-sounding woman who tells us to come to the top floor. We glide up the stairs along the gilded banisters and wordlessly exchange comments about all the bird décor. Every sound echoes, so we don't dare to speak in case the lady is waiting for us at the top and can hear every word we say. Ravens are everywhere, etched into everything, from the chandeliers that fly overhead to the ironwork bars on the windows looking out onto the street. The skylight brightens the stairwell so even the ribbons of dust seem to be dancing with an awareness that this is a house of mourning, one that's missing its daughter. I knew Mally's dad was rich, but this is different. This is glamorous. I don't know anyone else from the Scar born into this kind of opulence. Her mother was the most powerful fairy in Wonder, and the gifts people brought her in exchange for her attention are all over this place. No wonder Mally acts like she's superior. If I'd been raised with all this I would probably think I was superior, too.

I'm so busy trying to make the world bend into sense that Bella has to pull me back when we reach the top-floor landing.

"Holy toasters," she says. "What is that?"

I'm still trying to figure it out myself. I think before I speak, looking at the man splayed out across the bulk of the entrée. I'm lost for words so I say, "Holy toasters is right. That's the biggest man I've ever seen."

I take a step forward but Bella stops me. "Wait! Isn't there some saying about never waking a sleeping giant?"

"You're going to yank me to my death. Also, I think that's about babies."

She releases me. "Oh, right."

"Come on!" I nudge her up the last two marble stairs.

A small, well-cared-for tree sits in a pot on the landing. There's also a green, wordless welcome mat. More impressive than the sweet little entry to the penthouse apartment is the man who sits crumpled into an enormous chair outside the door. He's not exactly a giant the way you would think of it in a story, but he is massive compared to, say, me. He's got to be seven feet, with hands the size of pork roasts. My guess is he's not supposed to be napping right now, because he has a walkie-talkie in his pocket and a phone in his hand. Under his jacket I see the bulk of a holster. He must be some kind of bodyguard.

Bella clears her throat and the man only snores a touch and twitches.

The door to the apartment swings open and a woman with white hair tied in a severe bun pokes her head out.

"Anton!" the woman says.

The man opens his eyes and rubs at them, then straightens. "Magda! Oh golly, Magda, I am sorry." He looks at us. "Are you here with the caviar?"

"Caviar?" Magda scans us up and down. "You said you were with the Monarch Police. Detectives?" She places a hand on either hip and grimaces fiercely. "I'll have a look at your badges, please." She swats Anton on the shoulder. "And you! You should be ashamed of yourself."

"What? He kept me up all night, Magda. All night!"

She nods, face softening. "It's true he hasn't slept much the last few days without Miss Mally home. Troubling, troubling times." We move forward so we're within reach as she looks at both our badges. "Apologies. You look young for police."

"I suppose I've lost track of time," Anton says to no one in particular. Then he seems to remember something and he massages a temple. "I keep forgetting about our Mally girl. I go to sleep and it gets wiped clean, but this is the third morning I've woken up and she's not here. It's awful. Just awful. And who would dare? Who would do anything to that poor, sweet girl?"

Bella and I exchange a quick glance. This is a first, but it's nice to know someone actually likes Mally.

"I'll go and see that he's ready," Magda says. "Back in a moment." The sound of old-time music and a woman's singing wafts on to the landing.

"While she's gone we should go over the rules." Anton nods. "He has two. No recording him or taking any pictures of him, and no weapons in the house."

Bella hesitates. "That's not usually a thing we do. Our weapons are required to stay in our possession."

I don't mention I have only pepper spray, so it's not much of a loss for me. Anyway, when I remember Jack Saint in the station, it's of a soothing, sad presence, nothing threatening.

"I'm telling you, if you want to see him you'll put your weapons in this box along with the phones, and I will have them here when you get back."

I pull out my pepper spray and lay it on the table.

Bella gives me a look.

"We're breaking protocol for a good reason."

Bella lays her gun next to my things. "I hope you're right."

"The master will see you now," Magda says.

"G'luck." Anton takes a seat.

"And you," Magda says. "No sleeping."

"Yes, ma'am. Your wish is my command."

We pass through the threshold and Magda removes our coats and ushers us into a dim room covered mostly in velvet. Jack Saint is in a big brown leather easy chair, staring through his windows out above the Scar. The buildings are tall, though none taller than this one, so it's possible to see all the way to Miracle. It is an inarguably beautiful view. I might be hypnotised by it if not for the fact that Jack Saint is surrounded by birds. Ravens to be exact. They are huge, glossy and black. Three of them sit in the window sill cawing. They flap away, then come back. There must be a dozen of them, and the abandoned street below is so silent, all that's to be heard other than the music is the flapping of wings and incessant nattering.

Jack bobs his head in time to the music. "Beautiful, isn't it?" he says to the room, maybe to us, though he still hasn't looked our way, and it's hard to know if he's talking about the birds or the street or his apartment or the song. Hellion is on a perch next to him. I recognise him set apart from the others because he's bigger and has what looks like a ruff around his neck. Hellion spots us and caws aggressively.

"No, no, pet," Jack says. "They're not a threat." He finally turns his gaze on us and I nearly gasp. The toll the last twenty hours has taken on Jack Saint is shocking. He's still wearing the same clothes he had on at the station and has a profound stubble on his cheeks. His eyes, which last night seemed so kind and alive, have dulled and are bloodshot.

"Children?" He smiles ruefully. "My darling Chief Ito sent children to find my Mally?"

"With all due respect, we're not children," Bella says. "We're on this case because we're Legacy." She shows Jack Saint her mark. "Only Legacy can find Legacy in the Scar."

"My apologies," he says. "Grief has made me rude."

"I know Mally," I say, "or at least I've known who she is for a long time." I step closer to him. "She seems like someone who makes her own rules."

He nods. "Yes. That's how she is. She's so misunderstood. People fear her power. It's what has made this so difficult. She has been known to make people angry at times, and without her mother's guidance there are things I haven't been able to give her, things she needs. Fairies may not walk among us anymore, but she has fairy queen blood in her veins and that does something to a person."

Like gives her extra hostility and lack of reason and selfishness and meanness?

"I encourage her to soar," he says, "but just like the birds, she knows where home is."

Bella steps forward. "Sir, I'm so sorry to have to ask you some questions about Mally when you're clearly so distressed, but we'd like to get back to the business of finding your daughter."

He waves two ravens off a chair covered in gold brocade. "Please sit down."

Bella is almost comically dwarfed by the chair, and pulls her notepad from her satchel, adjusting her glasses and turning to the page she's looking for. Finally, she finds it and looks up. "I've done a comprehensive analysis based on Mally's last six months of bank statements. You're more than welcome to look at it."

Jack Saint shakes his head. "Not necessary. I'm aware of my daughter's finances."

"Well, sir, she may be a free spirit, but she seems to follow the same pattern nearly every day, at least according to her bank card."

"Yes, I believe that's so."

Bella reads from a list. "She's at the Tea Party for coffee every morning. Then to the bookstore."

"Yes," he says. "She favours philosophy. The Materialists."

"Then school, no lunch I could find, then Wonderland. I found table charges almost every day. She would leave there about midnight and then start all over the next day. Weekends I see she liked to shop on the strip. That's it." Bella looks up as though she's asked a question and is waiting for an answer.

Jack Saint strokes the feathers on one of his birds. "I wish I had been more of a disciplinarian. But you understand, she was always so upset. I got her every kind of help I could think of."

Something James said to me when we were in the Ever Garden is coming back to me now. I didn't even have the chance to open her file or I would have seen it. "Her mother died in the Fall?"

"She did, and sometimes I'm glad of it. My wife would not have done well in a world without magic." He looks at us. "I've done everything I can. After Mally's mother went down in the Fall, I swore I would keep Mally safe. She's all I have left. I made sure Mally's teeth were brushed and her clothes were clean. I made sure she ate all her greens. It didn't matter. I couldn't make her forget her mother. She appreciated me but I wasn't enough. What she really wanted was something I couldn't give her, some peace, some sense that things were going to be okay. I could never promise her that because that's not the world we live in, and I didn't want to lie to her about the things I could and couldn't control. But Mally always called. She always sent texts. She wandered, but never far, and she always had Hellion at her side and never missed a check-in time. Because of her trauma, she stayed close to home and followed a routine."

Mally. Trauma. I've always thought of her as being soulless, impervious to the things that make life hard… like feelings. But maybe Mally is just a hurt person like the rest of us.

"Come," Jack says, when Bella is done taking notes and has returned the notebook to her satchel. "I'll show you her room."

There is only one picture, and it's of Mally standing between her parents, both long and tall and thin, draped in black. Her mother has high cheekbones and a cruel mouth with a surprisingly delicate nose. Arrogance is written on every feature. I put the picture down and look around. The carpet is a warm beige, the walls a complementary cream colour. She has a dressing table with a marble top, covered in jewellery boxes and perfumes in crystal bottles, and there's a tall wooden perch next to her bed. The only other thing of note in the room is a large mural of black birds painted onto the wall behind her bed.

"May I?" I ask.

Bella is already in the wardrobe.

Jack nods.

I open the dressing table drawer to find make up perfectly organised, and clean brushes in a satin cloth. Everything in here speaks of affluence and comfort and care.

Bella holds up a silver laptop. "Mind if we take a look at what's on here? There could be something. Maybe she had acquaintances you didn't know about?"

"Please," Jack says. "I don't know the password."

"That's all right," Bella says. "I'm good with that sort of thing."

"Have you cleaned in here since she disappeared?" I ask. "Touched anything?"

"Hellion comes in here and perches on the window sill, so sometimes I leave the windows open, but other than that, Magda has only been in to vacuum and dust as she usually does."

"Everything is where it should be? You haven't noticed anything missing, have you?"

"I have not," Jack says.

It's true, all this room tells us is that Jack employs an excellent housekeeper. Maybe there's something on the computer, but overall, this has been fruitless.

Magda comes in, hovering at the doorway. "Excuse me, Mr Saint, but your caviar has arrived."

"Thank you, Magda," he says. "Tell Anton to come in and get off that damn landing. Would you make us some soup and sandwiches?"

"Yes, sir," she says, disappearing at once.

"We'll get out of your way," I say.

"Unless you have anything else you'd like to share with us," Bella says. "Anything at all you think might be important."

Jack hesitates. Bella sees it, too.

"Mr Saint?" I say.

Hellion tuts in his ear.

"They say people should always follow the money in a crime," Jack says. "Who has it. Who wants it. You know this."

I nod.

"There has been a crime here, and I've found that everything we do comes down to some type of greed, because with money comes power, and for some people that's all that matters. If you follow the money, maybe you will find Mally. That's what I'm trying to do on my end. But you keep those weapons of yours close, because if you start playing with people's money, you'll be gambling with your safety."

"We'll be fine, sir," Bella says, checking her phone. "We've got to get down to the station."

Before I can really think about it, I quickly grab a silver bracelet from the dressing table and slip it into my pocket. Something about it draws me in, like it's a real piece of Mally Saint, delicate, with a small knife dangling from its links.

My phone rings as we're headed back down the stairs. It's a number I don't recognise but I answer anyway.

"Yes?"

"Mary Elizabeth," a small voice says. "It's Morgana." Ursula's little sister.

"Morgie?"

"Yeah."

"What is it? Is everything okay?"

"No," she says. "Do you know where Ursula is? Ma had a doctor's appointment and Ursula didn't come home to take her. She never misses those. And then I tried to call her and her phone went straight to voicemail. That never ever happens. Mary, I think something's wrong."

Even though I just saw Ursula sleeping on my couch and there could be several reasonable explanations for her not checking in with her family, my heart falls into my shoe.

"Bella," I say, "I have to go. Right now."

TEN

ONCE I SOOTHE MORGIE ENOUGH TO GET HER off the phone, I call Urs and her phone goes straight to voicemail. I'm not too worried yet. Then I call Gia. She tells me Ursula left hours ago, so I call James but he hasn't seen her, either. He tries to tell me I shouldn't worry, that Ursula can take care of herself, but the truth is Ursula is only ever at four places: my house, her house, school or Wonderland, and she's usually with one of us.

We check Wonderland, but we don't see her there, so we leave. I'm so exhausted I fall asleep as soon as I get home.

When I wake up in the morning I try Ursula again, but there's still no answer. I'm definitely not going to school today. I do my best to keep my composure so Gia doesn't get worried, but it's not working. After talking to Morgana again and finding out Ursula didn't come home the night before, my vision fish-eyes and then implodes, and I'm caught between panic and fury as I go over every stupid mistake I made. I shouldn't have let her ditch school, or left her at my house, or gone so many hours without checking in with her. I call Dally Star to see if she ever showed up at Wonderland between the time I went in there and the time I went to sleep.

"Ursula?" he says. "Yeah, she was in here last night."

"Was she with anyone?"

"Well, I don't know, sweetheart, the place was packed. But I know I served her a Caterpillar, and then I don't remember seeing her after that."

"Okay, Dally, if you see her, tell her to charge her phone. And I'll need the footage from last night."

"Sure, sure. More footage. Happy to help."

The line goes dead and I try Ursula again.

You've reached Ursula. If you don't have anything interesting to say, please don't say anything at all. If you do, fascinate me after the tone.

"I know you're upset," Bella says, as the train ambles slowly uptown. We've both put our coats on (the weather is supposed to be bad uptown today). "But don't you think it's a little premature to assume Mally and Ursula are connected and to assume Ursula's actually missing? I mean *kidnapped* missing?"

"No, no, I don't," I say, folding my hands across my lap to keep from strangling Bella. Her talking is interrupting my thinking. There's something I'm missing here, something I'm not quite getting to. "Contrary to popular belief, Scar kids don't just up and leave the safety of their homes without any explanation."

"Okay, so what you're saying is Ursula is like Mally? No friends, does the same thing every day? Can reliably be found at any time?"

"No! She has tons of friends. She's loud and constantly

annoying people off, too, okay? But she has dirt on every single one of those people, so they'd have to think long and hard before doing something to her."

"So they both have enemies? That's what connects them?"

"Uh... no! What connects them is that they both go to Monarch High, they're both seventeen, neither of them listens to anyone else, and most important, they're both Legacy."

It's not until I say this that I know it's true. The fact that they're Legacy is important. The train rumbles on, picking up speed, and Bella and I pause our conversation, mostly due to the man sitting across from us and his interested stare. It's hard to remember to be careful when it comes to magic. He gets off at the stop before us, giving us each a stony look.

"What does it mean to be Legacy?" Bella says, after a minute.

"What? Why would you ask me a question like that? I don't know!"

"I'm asking honestly. Magic has been dead for nearly thirteen years. So what does it even mean now? Not all of us are descendants of important people. For some Legacy it just meant being able to shape shift or teleport."

"Legacy were a force for good. Most of the magic in the Scar was all about making dreams and wishes come true, about making things better for other people. Legacy made people feel good, gave people something to look forward to, kind of a net underneath them if things went really wrong. There's no safety net anymore." I let this settle in. "Legacy were the ones who were allowed to use magic and pass it out, to help people who couldn't help themselves and had no access to it. It's asking a lot for people to be okay with it being gone forever. No more wands or wings or magic lamps. We have to be okay with some anomalous weather patterns and a lake that can kill you if you dip one toe? I don't know, Bella. I don't know if that's ever going to happen."

"Maybe we didn't deserve that gift or that responsibility. Maybe there's a reason it got taken away." She lowers her voice. "Maybe people in the Scar shouldn't be trying so hard to get it back."

"What does any of this have to do with Ursula and Mally?"

"Maybe nothing. It's just what Jack Saint was saying about following the money and the greed. I mean, I hope you're wrong about everything and that Ursula bounds into her house and she's perfectly all right and it turns out she just spent the night at a friend's."

"She didn't." I say this with total certainty. "I know all her real friends. There's just me and James and Smee, and of the three of us I'm the only person she ever stays the night with. And Ursula is beyond addicted to her phone. She doesn't go ten minutes without checking her social media and taking a selfie. She's gone." Despair is going to consume me. I try to breathe. I cannot panic. Despair is the enemy of action. I can't let it have me. I have to keep a level head.

"So you think money and magic are why two teenagers are missing?" I ask.

She shakes her head. "Honestly, I don't know yet," she says, brows furrowed. "But I will."

The station is its usual chaotic self, but today I don't care. I will run Mona over if she tries to keep me from getting to the chief. Bella has me by the sleeve and has been telling me since we stepped out of the subway into the snow to calm down, and now as the chief's door is in sight, Tony, Bella's old partner, blocks our way.

His black hair is greased into a ponytail and he is practically flexing as he stands between us and Chief Ito.

"Well, hello there, ladies!" he says.

"Tony," Bella says tightly.

"Did you hear the news? They put the body parts together and they know who it is… was. Poor guy. In fact, I found the last piece myself, on the commuter train between the Scar and Midcity. Pretty impressive, wouldn't you say?" Bella inhales to answer him, but he blusters on. "I suppose you could say it was just coincidence since I had to go to the Scar to interview the kid who found the part by the Tea Party, but it was genius when I spotted the wrapped-up box and got to it first."

"Sounds very impressive, Tony," Bella says. "Now, if you wouldn't mind…"

"So I was thinking," he says, sparing me a glance, "maybe you and I could duck over to get some dinner later, since you're here."

"I'm working, Tony," she says. "Something happened and I—"

"Sure, sure," he interrupts. "Chasing after that Scar heiress. How's that going? Any luck?"

His smug face tells me he knows perfectly well we haven't had any luck.

"So, Tony," I say.

"Yeah, kid?" He looks down at me indulgently.

"We need to get into the chief's office, and you're standing in our way."

"Yeah?" He looks at me blankly.

"And as far as I can tell, you're trying to hit on Bella and she has absolutely zero interest in ever going out with you, except you won't absorb that when she says it to you nicely because you absolutely cannot conceive that a woman would not want to date you. So since she's being too nice right now, let me clear things up for you. Bella doesn't want to date you. She doesn't even want to talk to you. She's never going to dinner with you, and the fact that you persist is harassment." At this he blanches. "So get. Out. Of. Our. Way."

"You know what?" he says, taking several steps back. "I was trying to be nice, but the two of you are a joke. You're never going to get anything done, and watching the two of you try to be taken seriously is pathetic."

"Thanks for your assessment of our abilities, Tony. Really insightful," Bella says brightly, then yanks on my sleeve and pulls me into the corner by our abandoned desks. "Thanks for that." She sniffs and raises her nose into the air imperiously. "Now, come on, enough dawdling. We need to be careful and considerate about how we approach the chief. She commands respect and she's not going to respond well if we barge into her office and—"

"Bella," I say, blood still pumping hard with the effort of not attacking Tony full throttle. "I don't have time to talk right now. I need to find Ursula. I need the chief to approve more resources. I need her to understand there's something bigger than just one person going missing or running away in the Scar."

"Okay," Bella says. "All I'm saying is that we should make a plan."

"There's no time for plans," I say, and push past her to open the door to the chief's office.

I burst in as she's meeting with two guys I recognise as senior detectives but don't personally know. She looks brighter than she did the other night. Less tired, but not at all pleased by the interruption.

"Yes?" she says.

"Oh goodness, no." Mona comes out from behind her desk and tries to shoo us from the room.

"I just need to talk to you for one minute," I say.

"I am in a meeting and everyone only needs to talk to me for one minute. You can wait your turn."

"I can't." I force my way past Mona.

The chief presses her lips together. Before she can kick me out I say, "My best friend's gone. She goes to Monarch, too. Her name's Ursula. She's got a sick mom and a little sister who depend on her and now she's missing. She can't be missing, you understand?"

"Mary," Bella says in a warning voice from beside me. I can barely hear her. I can't register her words. All I can see or feel is that Ursula isn't where she's supposed to be and that means she's not okay. What if she's being hurt? What if someone is torturing her?

"We need more resources," I say. "Put more officers in the Scar. Have them go door-to-door. There are so many places she and Mally could be—"

The chief puts up her hand, signals the detectives to leave. My chest is heaving.

"Miss Heart, are you giving me orders?"

"I'm just saying my friend deserves as much attention as Mally Saint. Just because Mally's rich doesn't mean she should get all the focus while Ursula just *vanishes* and no one does a thing!"

Bella pinches me lightly and it's just enough to slow me down and help me get hold of my breath. "No, ma'am," Bella says. "Mary Elizabeth was definitely not giving you orders, ma'am. She is making a request. She's just a little overwrought today."

Mona closes the door so we're enclosed in her office once again. Only now does it truly sink in how out of my depth I am.

"That's very good to hear, Officer Loyola, because you know how much I do not appreciate taking orders."

"She doesn't like it at all," Mona says.

"So, now, Miss Heart, if you would please take a moment to gather yourself, you may start from the beginning."

"Stay in your lane," Bella says, nearly inaudibly.

"I believe there is a serial kidnapper in the Scar," I begin. "My best friend, Ursula, has been missing since last night. She lives in the same neighbourhood as Mally Saint. They are the same age and both attend Monarch High."

"Is that all?" the chief says, looking even more irritated than she did a few minutes ago.

"Well…"

"So if I'm understanding correctly – and please excuse any confusion as I was having a strategy meeting regarding the organised crime ring that's taking over Monarch right now – you'd like me to put my best officers on finding a friend who didn't call home when I'm close to cracking the Mad Hatter case and need all hands on deck for that."

"But—"

"And you'd like me to do this on a good-faith hunch that your friend has been kidnapped, who I'm certain is of unimpeachable character and who has been missing since what time?"

"Midnight," I say, seeing all the holes in my theory as they must appear to her.

"Midnight," she repeats. "Not even twenty-four hours. So, to recap, you'd like me to redistribute my resources as police chief to look for a girl who's probably not missing at all."

I can't answer. I know I'm right, but I also know there's no way for me to convince the chief. She sighs. "Mary Elizabeth, I understand your stress levels are high. I can even understand how you might make some misguided connection between your friend and Mally Saint, but I'm sure she'll be home safe and sound before you can make it back to the Scar."

I wish that were true, but I *know* it's not, and the chief's certainty, counter to mine, is dangerous. I don't know what I had expected; maybe that the chief and I were somehow so interwoven by fate and our mutual experience of life in the Scar and loss and her involvement in solving my parents' death that she would see me as something beyond the less-than-rookie I am. I am foolish, and I feel it in every nerve. I am foolish, but I am also right, and I can't let Ursula pay the price for the stupidity with which I approached the chief.

"Please just let me look for her," I say.

The chief gazes at me unflinchingly.

"Please let me investigate whether or not there's a connection… if she's not there when I get back to the Scar. I would be so grateful to you… again."

For a moment I see something human appear on her face, but it disappears as quickly as it came. "Unfortunately, I can't allow you to become involved in a case that close to you. It's a conflict of interest and a waste of taxpayer funds."

Now would probably be a bad time to remind her that my internship is unpaid.

"Your energy needs to remain on the primary objective of finding Mally Saint. Please tell your friend's mother to go through the appropriate channels and file a police report if she hasn't come back once the twenty-four hours is at its end. And I'd like you to schedule a meeting with Dr Tink. She can determine whether you're stable enough to continue working on this case."

Great. My entire life depends on my extremely quirky therapist assessing me properly. The thing is, I am stable enough to handle this. I need to find Ursula. I don't care what the chief says.

"Yes, ma'am."

She looks me over, like she can hear the lie in my voice, but I don't let my facial expression change at all.

"And one more thing, Miss Heart."

"Ma'am?"

"If you ever burst into my office again uninvited or have the audacity to speak to me in that tone of voice again, I will have you tossed out of the building and you will never be allowed through its doors again. Are we understood?"

"Yes, ma'am," I say. But I'm thinking, *You can say whatever you want and I'm going to do whatever I want and that's how it's going to be.* I'm feeling something new bubbling up to the surface, and I don't even know if I'm ready to look at it, but right then I don't like the chief at all, and there's this little voice inside me that's saying I don't even know who I am if I'm not the Mary Elizabeth Heart who worships Chief Ito.

She turns to Bella, eyes all warning black glitter. "Officer Loyola, keep her on a leash. I'll need reports on your progress by

Monday morning, so have a productive rest of your week."

"Ma'am," we say in unison.

When we leave the chief's office, Bella rubs my back and I shake her off. "Please don't," I say.

I'm still furious with myself for losing my composure like that, and so upset I blew my chance to figure out what's happened to Ursula.

"I just have to file the reports for today and I can come help you look for her. We'll find her… together." Bella goes over to her desk and sits down, opening her laptop and taking out her notes. She looks at me and smiles a little worriedly, then goes back to her screen.

I don't say goodbye to her, just slip out as soon as she's immersed in what she's doing.

And with that, I'm free. I run to the train, leaving Bella and Midcity behind. I know this internship is the path to the things I want, but these people aren't going to help me now, and I don't want Bella involved in this piece of my life.

I need to get to James and find my best friend.

ELEVEN

THE NIGHT IS FRUITLESS. I CALL URSULA'S phone again and again, just to hear the sound of her voice.

If you don't have anything interesting to say, don't say anything at all. If you do, fascinate me after the tone.

James and I go to Wonderland and we sit there for hours, waiting for Ursula because we don't know what else to do. I can't bear the thought of going to her house, we've already been all over her neighbourhood, and James has ears to the ground everywhere. He deals with it by playing pool, aggressively smashing the balls into each other so hard I think they're going to come apart. We both watch the door every time it opens, hoping it will be Ursula. I'd take her dirty and wounded and even starved and thirsty if she would just come through that door.

Smee and the rest of James's boys spend all night patrolling for Ursula. James even lets them take his car, and after Wonderland is closed we walk for hours, checking every corner and alley, James stopping to ask everyone on the street. The Scar is the same as always: balmy, palm trees swaying above us, people in tank tops and short skirts and high heels, dead magic all around us. We get home so late Gia is already almost done with her business day. James sits with her awhile. I keep looking to the couch where Ursula was asleep just yesterday. I should have held her there. I should have paid more attention. I don't even remember our last conversation. Something about spice cake, I think, but I don't know. I was so excited about the Mally case I have no idea what was going on with her.

I've been a bad friend and a bad person, selfish beyond reason. I've taken everything I have for granted and now it's being taken away. I keep wanting to tell Ursula about how Ursula is missing. I don't know if I can survive this.

Finally I go to the couch and lay my head just where she had hers, hoping something of her essence will slip into me, tell me where she is. I can't stop thinking about all the bad things that could be happening to her right now. James sinks down next to me, pulls me into his chest, and after a while I fall asleep holding him so tightly I'm surprised he can breathe at all. I don't want to take anything for granted ever again, and I hope if I hold on to James tight enough, he won't disappear, too.

By the next morning, when I'm in Dr Tink's chair because I have no idea what else to do, I'm thinking there's a chance I'm losing it.

I try to focus on Dr Tink, who sits across from me in a brown recliner, which has the effect of making her look like a plant. She has cropped blonde hair and small features on a heart-shaped face, and is in a fitted jacket and tight army-green trousers. She's bouncing her leg over her knee, waiting for me to answer something, but I don't know what it is. I do know in order to appear sane I should be more enthusiastic and as engaged as possible.

"Mary Elizabeth."

"Yes?"

"I know you haven't slept properly—"

"I have." The heat rises through me. "I'm sleeping literally all the time and you have no idea and you just think because I have a couple of measly circles under my eyes—"

Dr Tink cuts me off. "Anger is a defence mechanism, Mary Elizabeth. I have the records from the health app on your phone. You're running on a total of ten hours in the last three nights, only one and a half of those in the last twenty-four hours."

I forgot she had that information. I slump back in my seat waiting for whatever lecture she's about to give me. We've been meeting once a week for the last two months since I got this internship, and even though it's mostly supposed to be just supportive in case I run into stressful situations here at the station, she keeps pushing me to talk about my past, like she's convinced it's the key to something.

"Have you given any more consideration to what we talked about last time?" she says.

Last time was another lifetime ago, and I can't remember.

"About?"

"About your family? Have you given any thought to whether you're ready to talk about what happened that day?"

"I mean... I'm sorry, but what does that have to do with anything?" I say. "Everyone loses people." I don't know why she would make out my circumstances as especially traumatic. She's

Legacy, and everyone knows she lost a brother in the Fall.

She looks up at me as though startled, a flash of pain splitting through her cheerful veneer. Then she recalibrates. "Mary Elizabeth, it may be so that you don't think it matters, but it's also true that if you don't begin to connect to your own experiences, they will continue to control you, because whether you know it or not, that's what's happening. You are a series of reactions. Wouldn't you like to be more in control of the things that happen to you?"

I scoff. "Why would I hope for that when it's an impossibility? Things happen. They happen to us and we have to take it. Things are given and things are taken away and all we can do is get really good at riding the storm. So, yes, I'm reacting because life is happening and there's nothing else I can do."

Dr Tink looks lost in that brown chair right now, like it's eating her up. "I think you don't want to revisit that pain."

I lean forward. "I revisit it *all the time*. It's with me constantly." My voice cracks as I finish my sentence and I swallow it back.

Tink lets the air grow heavy between us, waiting for me to speak. When I don't, she says, "I'm going to recommend a leave of absence from your internship. I don't think it's good for you right now. You need some rest, some self-care."

"No, no, please don't!" I make myself sit upright and focus on her words. "You don't understand." Then I get it. I have to do what she says or let this dream of being a detective go right now, and while I currently hate the chief and feel like I'm useless in almost every way, if I storm out of here, I'll regret it in the morning. "Okay," I say. "I will tell you what happened, even though I don't think it's going to help or make any difference at all."

"Okay, Mary Elizabeth," Tink says. "When you're ready."

I close my eyes. I remember my mother. She was in a bad mood and she was wearing red. Her hand felt cool against mine.

"Good," Dr Tink says. "Now, tell me."

I don't open my eyes because I don't want to. If I do, I'll lose this image of my mother, the feeling of the day on my skin. I can't remember ever being this close to the memory, which has always felt far away and distorted. But now it's right here. *It's the blue light*, something whispers. *It's brought you so much closer to yourself.*

"My mother was mad, or at least annoyed. She was wearing a red sundress with little white hearts on it."

"Why was she mad?"

"Because my dad was sick and so was Mirana and she had stuff to do. She wasn't going to be able to do it because she was going to have to spend all day taking care of them. We held hands. She walked me to school and the whole time she was saying how she was glad I wasn't sick yet but I would probably be very soon and so her whole week would be ruined."

"Do you remember anything else about walking to school?"

"Just that the sun was shining and all the clouds were shaped like cookies."

"And then?"

"She kneeled down and rubbed the top of my head and her eyes were so blue and her hair was so red and the hearts on her dress seemed like they were dancing." I remember something. "Dancing. We learned how to square dance that day. Do-si-do."

"Everyone has to endure that at some point," Dr Tink says.

"And then the police came."

"Okay."

"They came and got me and took me to the station. They didn't tell me what was happening for a long time, so I just watched everyone answering phones and typing into computers and rushing around. Then a detective came and sat next to me. I remember she smelled good. She took me into a room and she told me. She said my aunt was coming to get me and I would be going home with her."

"What else did she tell you, Mary?"

I shudder. Something oozy and long dormant is trying to push its way out of my mouth. It tastes metallic.

"She told me…" I can feel my body trembling. I remember being in that room with so much white, a TV monitor hung in one corner, a mirror along the breadth of a wall. "She told me my family had been killed, that some bad person had gone into our apartment and found my dad and Mirana sick in bed and he had killed them and then my mom, and then he had left. And I was thinking it was so strange I had been learning how to square dance while someone had been killing my family."

"Go deeper. How were you feeling?"

"Mirana. I was thinking about her. About the blue penguin she carried around with her everywhere. I was wondering where it was and if she got to hold it when… when he…" I can't breathe. I reach for my chest, which is tightening so I can't breathe.

"It's okay, Mary," Tink says. "You can do this. When you have these memories, count backwards from ten to one. Just focus on the numbers. Go on."

"Now?" I say.

"Yes! Yes, now."

"Okay." I inhale. "Ten, nine, eight, seven, six, five, four, three, two, one." I try to count slowly, to steady myself against the shivery feeling left in the wake of my memories.

"Good. You feel better?"

"Yes," I say. "You know, I actually do." And it's true, something about reliving that day has made it seem less frightening and ominous.

"Can you go on? Tell me what happened next?"

I take one full breath, let my lungs fill, then empty completely. "Yes, I can."

"Okay," Dr Tink says. "Whenever you're ready."

I sink back into the memory, and this time I have more distance from it, enough to feel safe like an observer in the room instead of the person it was happening to.

"I was thinking how strong my dad was. He could pick up a piano, so I didn't understand how anyone could have done that to him. How could a single person have overpowered him and proven him fallible? It was almost impossible for me to conceive that could be the case. The detective held my hand and she looked me straight in the eye and she told me she was going to get the person who did this to my family, that the only reason the bad man had been able to do what he had was that my father was so sick. He wasn't himself. He couldn't have lifted a piano that day. She told me she was going to make sure the killer spent the rest of his life behind bars. She waited with me until Gia got here to pick me up. Here to the station. In this building. Everything happens here."

My throat aches. I want to stop talking.

"And the detective."

"Chief Ito." I open my eyes and let the room come back into

focus, the collection of tea and cookies in the corner, the books about getting the love you deserve, the row of succulents along the window with its blinds drawn tight. "She wasn't chief then," I say. "My hand went from my mother's to hers to Gia's that day."

"Yes."

"The chief took care of me. And then there was the press conference when she found him. I presented her with the award in front of all those people."

I hear the pop of flashes, see how they blinded me, how much I loved being centre stage in front of all those people. It was the first time I thought, *I want to do this.*

"I was ten. I hid my face in the chief's skirt. She kept me safe." I pause. I *did* expect to be someone special to the chief, which is why the way she treated me yesterday offended me so much. I may have had no contact with her until recently, but I was there, orbiting around her, waiting for her to notice me. And then she did and it never ever occurred to me that once she turned her gaze my way she would retract it. I thought when she saw me and recognised my abilities I would be embraced, that we were connected, like I was some kind of surrogate daughter from afar or something. It's such a joke. How many hundreds of kids has the chief helped by now? How many hands has she taken? How many eyes has she looked into and made promises? It's her job. I'm only the most minor piece of it. I mean nothing to her.

Dr Tink hands me a tissue, but I don't need it. My heart is too heavy for tears.

"It took me a long time to realise what the chief said was true, that my dad had such a bad fever he was too weak to defend himself. And the man who did it. He didn't even care. He didn't feel anything. It was just another Legacy hate crime. He didn't even think of my parents and my sister as people." I look at Tink. "I never got to go back home. I know now it was such a bloodbath no one wanted me in there with the crime scene tape and the carnage. But I just wanted to go home. I always wanted to go home. And then I found James and Ursula, and Gia. It's not the same as before, but it's something. It's some kind of home."

Tink nods. "This is something we have to do in the face of tragedy. We can't heal and be whole in the same way we were before the event, but we can build bridges over the gaps we have inside us." Tink looks at the pad of paper on her lap, looks upwards as though trying to find answers in the air above her head. "And how do you feel now, Mary Elizabeth?"

I think about this, about how honest to be. "I feel… *furious*. I feel vengeful. I feel like everything that's happening and that's been happening since I was born has been unjust and there needs to be justice."

For a second I think I've said exactly the wrong thing and she will recommend a leave or another candidate for the internship, but she only nods.

"I know Ursula is missing," she says, "and although I hear the circumstances are somewhat different from the case you're working on, you believe there's a connection."

"Yeah." A sob threatens to break through and I can't let it because if I do, everything is going to come out and there's too much. "Sometimes it feels like the world is ending," I say, when I know I'm strong enough to speak. "Sometimes it feels like it's been ending my whole life."

She leans forward. "Say more about that."

I struggle through my desire to clam up and look out her tenth-storey window to the wide expanse of grey and the triangle of the building next door. "It seems like when magic died it took the soul out of everything, and now anything is possible and everything is happening. It's like the whole world is being pulled into some kind of sinkhole."

Tink taps her pen on her chin, her bright green eyes twinkling.

"I know that's not what's actually happening, but it feels like it. And so, yeah, Ursula is one small thing that makes me feel like the world isn't going anywhere. Her disappearing just makes me feel like every crazy thought I have is true. I'll sleep," I say. "Whatever you want. But please make the recommendation for me to keep my internship. Please."

Tink glances at her watch. This office is like a factory for disturbed cops. I'm sure she's got more serious clients to see, people whose partners were killed in the line of duty or whatever.

She blinks. "Don't you wish you could just believe and make it all okay? Wish on a star or clap your hands hard enough to put everything back where it should be? Ah, well. That's not the world we live in, is it?" She sighs. "Still, I want you to promise to do it twice a day and to get a minimum of six hours of sleep. You must attend school and do what's required there. And remember, any violent outbursts, lack of self-control, or further signs of stress and I'll recommend you take a break."

"Thank you! I'll be so good. I'll be excellent!"

"And, Mary? Just remember, sometimes extending a hand to someone can make a huge difference to them. When you're always defending yourself from something you think is coming round the next corner, when you think the world is against you, there isn't much of a chance for the good stuff to come through. It's okay to be furious if your fury is aimed in the right direction. Just don't let it eat up what's soft in you."

"Okay," I say. "The universe is not my enemy despite all evidence to the contrary. Got it!"

She smiles, and scrawls her signature at the bottom of my assessment update.

"You did good work today, Mary Elizabeth. Deep work. Take care of yourself, and don't do anything foolish."

"I won't."

"And Mona told me to send you back in. I guess there's been a report filed about Ursula, and Officers Colman and Mahony have been assigned to the case." She watches as I absorb the news. Ursula is an official missing person now, and people are investigating it. Someone has been assigned to the case. It's just not me. "Isn't that good news?" she asks. "She's being listed as a missing person. That means it'll be investigated."

"Yes, it's good." Not as good as Ursula coming home. I shake off the hurt and jealousy, and worse, the knowledge that if this case is being investigated by a separate set of detectives, no one is seeing the connection I'm certain is there.

"Good," she says. "Remember to do *your* work, your case, and to take care of yourself and stay out of danger."

"I promise," I say.

She gives me a warm handshake and I push back a twinge of guilt.

Even as I make the promise, I know it's a lie.

TRANSCRIPT FROM THE RECORDED INTERVIEW
OF MARY ELIZABETH HEART
REGARDING THE CASE OF MISSING PERSON
URSULA ATLANTICA

Interview taken by Detectives Colman and Mahony
at Monarch City Main Precinct

Mahony: Mary Elizabeth, for the record, you are an intern here at Monarch Main Precinct and are currently on a case looking for the whereabouts of Mally Francine Saint?

Mary: That's right.

Mahony: And you are a friend of Ursula Atlantica?

Mary: Yes.

Mahony: And can you tell us about your relationship to Ursula?

Mary: She's my best friend.

Mahony: How long would you say she's been your best friend?

Mary: I've known her since first grade, so eleven years. We met after the Great Death.

Mahony: And for the record, can you confirm you're both Legacy?

Mary: Yes. Yes, we're both Legacy.

Mahony: Can you tell us when you last saw Ursula?

Mary: Thursday afternoon.

Mahony: So that's two days ago.

Mary: Yes.

Mahony: And where was she when you last saw her?

Mary: She was at my apartment. I left her there to go to my internship. She was going to go home to check on her mother and sister. I guess she never went.

Colman: We're still waiting to obtain footage, but it seems Ursula went to Wonderland instead of going home as she told you she was going to. Can you explain why she might do that?

Mary: She could have been meeting someone?

Colman: Is that a question?

Mary: I don't know. I don't know what she could have been doing. I was working.

Mahony: What Colman is asking is if you know she was meeting someone that afternoon.

Mary (pause): No. I don't know why she went to Wonderland.

Colman: And when you saw her last, did she seem depressed, distraught in any way?

Mary: No, just tired.

Colman: And is it true that your apartment is located next to Miracle Lake, a popular site for suicide?

Mary: She didn't do that! She would never do that.

Mahony: Sorry. Sorry to upset you. It's something we have to consider.

Colman: We need to ask you something and we're hoping you'll be honest. In conducting some interviews, we've found that Ursula had quite the side business, and it made her a few enemies. She was apparently blackmailing several of her teachers, the school principal and the, uh, owner of the corner bodega. It's been harder to gather information about this from kids your age. They get a little squirrely around us. So maybe you can tell us exactly what was going on with Ursula's illegal activities.

Mary: I don't know much. I never thought of it as illegal.

Colman: You thought blackmail was legal?

Mary: Well no, but…

Colman: Seems like maybe plenty of people would have benefited from having her gone.

Mary: No, everyone loves her.

Mahony: I'm afraid that's not so. Not so at all.

Mary (hesitant): I don't know anything.

Colman: And your boyfriend?

Mary: What about him?

Colman: No, nothing. Just his father.

Mahony: Nothing we need to discuss at the moment. Here's my card. Just make sure you stay in touch. I know you'll do the right thing if you hear of anything.

Colman: And if you don't do the right thing, it's not only a breach of your contract with this precinct, it's obstruction of justice.

Mary: Can I go?

Colman: Please do.

Mahony: Stay in touch, Miss Heart.

TWELVE

"THEY WERE AWFUL, JAMES. COLMAN AND Mahony. They asked all these questions and you could tell they were anti-Legacy and they made Ursula sound like she was totally worthless and it was to be expected she'd be kidnapped or taken out or something. They made it sound like it was her own fault." James and I are roaming in his car, looking for signs of Ursula while the boys keep their eyes out at Wonderland. I can't go there and face Dally and all his prying questions, especially when I don't have any answers for him. I don't know where Mally is. I don't know where Ursula is. I know nothing.

After my epic meltdown in front of the chief yesterday, Bella let me off the hook for casework today while she did some digging into the Mally Saint case. But I can't just take the rest of the day off. I'm too restless.

James pulls over in front of Mally's apartment building. The birds are flying overhead against the night, and a cornmeal-yellow light can be seen upstairs in Jack Saint's apartment. I hope he's having a better time up there than I'm having down here.

We get out and sit on the bonnet of the car.

"Come here," James says.

I scoot into him and we sit for a few minutes, both of us distracted by our rushing minds.

"James," I say.

"Yeah?"

I want to ask him about the blue light. It's been hanging between us since Wednesday night, and ever since then life seems to have accelerated so there hasn't even been time to talk about something that has to be monumentally important. Ever since we were little, James has been saying he would find a way to bring magic back, that he would use his intuition to do it. He may not officially be a Magicalist, but he has the same ideas. Magic is dormant and, like oil or any other natural resource, can be harvested if it can be found. And now it seems like he's found it. That's huge.

James draws me in closer. "You want me to tell you everything?"

"I don't know, do I? We've never kept secrets from each other before."

"If I told you everything, you would wish I hadn't. There's a mandatory reporting law for anything even remotely magical in the Scar, and you're a cop. I'm not going to say anything else." He peers around us at the empty street. "It's up to you, Mary. If you want me to tell you everything, I'll tell you. But I won't be able to take it back once I do."

Being away from James is hard. Going to work, not knowing what he's doing with his boys, what they're up to, if they're doing something dangerous. But being close to him is hard, too – looking into his brown eyes, those long lashes, not having the words to tell him he's the only thing I have left other than a dream to make this city into something we can both live with.

"No," I say. "Don't tell me. Not yet. But I do have something." I pull out Mally's bracelet and hand it to James. "It's Mally's. I thought maybe you could help me. Use your intuition, maybe your blue light? I have this, too." I pull the ring from my finger. "It used to be Ursula's. Do you think you might be able to find them with these?"

"I have no idea, but I'll see what I can do."

My thoughts turn back to Ursula. Those cops don't care about her. I need to go to her house, find her naughty list, talk to Morgana and their mother. I need to see what I can find in her room, something those moron detectives might have missed. I'm forbidden from it officially, but no one can stop me from going to my best friend's house for a visit.

"Hey," James says. "It's going to be okay. It's the worst not knowing where she is, but I think she's all right."

"Think?"

"I would feel it."

I would feel it, too. I know what he's saying is true.

"Maybe my Trace will send me another dream."

"Maybe," James says with a yawn. "We'll find her."

There's a loud caw and the swirl of feathers as Hellion lands on the lamp post next to us.

"What is that?" James says. "Is that Mally's bird?"

I recognise Hellion by his ruff, and he looks right at me and lets out an angry accusatory cry. "What do you want, bird?"

He makes a series of nattering noises.

"You go look for her," I say.

He tilts his head to one side.

"I can't find her, so you go." This is ridiculous, I know. This bird can't understand what I'm saying. At least I don't think he can. The way he's looking at me I'm not so sure. "Go find Mally and bring her home."

He lets out a long, loud caw and then disappears into the night in a fury of flapping wings.

James lets out a soft, incredulous laugh. "If I didn't know better, I'd say that bird is following your instructions."

"Don't judge me," I say. "Those Midcity morons aren't going to find Ursula, and apparently I'm not going to find Mally, either. Hellion has as good a chance as anyone else."

I remember the chief's warning and Bella's words about staying in my lane. This is the most I can do for my best friend and it doesn't feel like nearly enough.

All I can do is sit on the bonnet of a car staring into darkness, hoping Ursula will emerge from it and come home to me.

Monday morning when James picks me up for school, Smee climbs into the back seat without any complaint or whining, a sign of just how low everyone is feeling. When we get into the usually loud and chaotic hallway at Monarch High, it's silent. There's no fighting and no bickering or banter. Dreena is wearing a black armband and waves to me mournfully. Stone plucks out a disjointed tune on his bass. It's like Ursula and Mally were two forces of nature giving all of us energy or something to watch or push against, and now there's nothing but a void.

It's torture. No Mally. No Ursula. A profound sense of unrest fills the hallway. Legacies aren't being their usual boisterous selves, and the Narrows skulk around the halls looking paranoid and ready for a fight.

In History we all shuffle into our groups, but without Ursula in the room, it feels cavernous and too quiet. No one says anything to me, but I can feel myself being watched, especially by Lucas, but even he doesn't have anything to say.

"This morning," Mr Iago says when everyone is settled, "I'd like everyone to get laptops and fill out the survey about inclusivity you'll find in the virtual classroom. Because Monarch High is located in a predominantly Legacy neighbourhood, city officials, including Mayor Triton, want to make sure the school is unbiased in its approach to education." He clears his throat. "If you would be so kind as to give your feedback for this class, I would be grateful. It's a requirement. Following, if you would please read chapter eight and then do the assignment at the end, that will be the day's work. You can stay at your tables, but there will be, uh, no discussion. Not today." He goes to sit at his desk but then stands again. "I should also mention that if anyone is having trouble with recent events, or has been having thoughts of um, self-harm, I have some pamphlets here, kindly provided by Dreena, and I encourage all of you to seek help if you need it."

"Oh man," James says from across the room. "Are you trying to say… Do you think Ursula and Mally are suicides?"

"Well, why not, Crook?" Lucas says dully. "Not like they had much to look forward to."

Smee leans forward. "Say the word, Cap. You want me to end this loser?"

"No," James says, "but someday when you aren't expecting it, I'll get you for that one."

Katy raises her hand as she says, "Teacher, did you hear that? Smee and James threatened Lucas."

"Well, uh…"

"I wanted to make sure you caught that." She looks at James pointedly. "Maybe whoever is taking Scar kids is one of them. Maybe someone hiding in plain sight."

"Students, please!" Iago says over the rumble in the room, but the truth is, the fighting is a relief. I'll take it over the aching silence.

James looks as though he's paying attention to what's in front of him but I can feel him focusing on me, all the questions circling his mind. Ursula wouldn't jump into Miracle Lake, would she? Would Mally? Ursula's been stressed-out about her mom and Morgana, sure, but she also loves life more than almost anyone I can think of. She just sees it differently than most people, like a game that's meant to be won. Jumping into Miracle would not be winning.

"It's so much quieter at school these days, don't you think?" Katy leans forward to talk to Josey, one of the other Narrows. But Josey likes us. She even tries to pass with stick-on Legacy markings. She shrugs her shoulders and tries to focus on the screen in front of her. "It's just so much more pleasant without a certain someone here. So much less trashy." Katy sucks on whatever drink is in the white to-go cup she's carrying. I would bet money it's something way too sweet that sits on your tongue long after it should be gone.

I'd like to rip her tongue out of her head, but I have the chief's and Tink's warnings ringing through my mind. No physical violence.

"Katy, don't," Josey says without much force.

"I'm not trying to be aggressive, I'm just telling the truth. It just smells so much better without Ursula around. Because she's trashy. Get it?" She giggles.

"That's enough," Lucas says quietly.

"But she is!"

I can't take it anymore. I can't take one more second of Katy moving her mouth and sound coming out. "Listen to me, you little idiot," I say. "You don't talk about Ursula again. Ever."

Murmurs erupt all around us.

"We have two choices here," Mr Iago says, raising his voice from behind his desk. "We can set aside our differences and do the assignments silently so our very tired and emotionally exhausted teacher can recover, or we can go outside and you can do laps for the next sixty minutes. Which do you choose?"

Katy sniffs at me and I sniff back, but we both go back to the survey.

Do you feel all factions are represented in the classroom?

Do you feel you can speak freely in the classroom and your perspective will be heard?

Do you feel you know your teacher's political opinions?

I don't know how to answer these questions, so I read them over and over. What are they asking? Why are they asking it?

My hand flops onto the chair. The minutes tick by, one after another. It gets harder and harder to maintain focus and I stop trying to follow the questions, and then from across the room I can hear James's alligator watch. *Tick.*

Tick.

Tick.

Tick.

Tick.

I want to tell James to quiet his watch down, that it's making so much noise I can't think, but I find I can't use my voice. When I try to move my hands, to speak, I can't. I turn my head towards James. It takes one million years. Every millimetre stretches out into an easy but relentless effort, like my head is an unwieldy balloon and is difficult to control because it could float off my shoulders anytime.

James is trying to talk to me, but his voice is coming out in a long whisper. His words aren't right. I don't even know which language he's speaking. Something is happening. My arms tingle, but I can't move them at all.

A humming starts up, so I strain towards it, making huge efforts to straighten my head again.

Mally Saint is in the seat where Katy was a few minutes ago. She's as regal as ever, thin shoulders thrown back proudly, hair slicing across one cheek. She looks as though she may have lost a little weight and is even more gaunt. She freezes for a second when she makes direct eye contact with me. She is terrifying and casts a shadow across the classroom. She begins to hum again and this time it shakes the whole room, so everything vibrates. I can only look at her and I can only hear the tune she's humming.

She stops, suddenly. No one is looking at us. It's like we're not here at all.

Mally nods her head towards James. "You'd better watch him," she says.

I try to speak and no words come out. I don't want her to look at him. Her nails are longer than I remember, painted a deep blood red, and they tap the top of the desk, one at a time.

"This isn't as bad as I thought." She leans back in the desk. "It still hurts to get here, but life is pain anyway, isn't it?"

I need to talk to her, but I'm mute. I could cry from frustration if I could even move.

She leans close over the desk, gets close enough to whisper in my ear. "When I made my choice between my head and my heart, it was easy. Who wants to feel? And then they took it. They took it. Just. Like. This."

She presses her fingers into my chest like she did the last time I dreamed about her, rips through the skin. But then she looks over my head and pulls her finger back.

"No," she says. I've never seen Mally look afraid before. I want to see what she's afraid of.

I wish I could turn my head.

"Leave me alone!" Her eyes dart towards me and she starts talking superfast. "Ursula escaped. She's gone to the only place they can't get her. You have to tell her to come back. She has to come back or they're going to—" And then, as though someone invisible and strong is pulling her by the feet, she is yanked out of the chair. She slaps against the plastic seat and whacks heavily against the floor, and then she slides along, head lolling to the side, eyes unblinking and open. She is dragged out of the classroom door, leaving a trail of sticky blue blood in her wake.

That's when I manage to scream.

I'm on the floor and can still hear the last of the echo of my own voice.

"Are you okay?" James looms over me, one hand under my neck, a look of pure panic on his face. "Mary, are you okay? Say something."

"Mally," I manage, breathing hard.

"Miss Heart," Mr Iago says. "Lucas, go get the nurse."

"Hardly," Lucas says.

"How many fingers am I holding up?" James says, shooting Lucas a dirty look I can see even through my haze.

"Two fingers," I tell James. "What happened?"

"I think you fell asleep. I don't know. You looked like you were nodding out, so I was trying to tell you to wake up and you started screaming."

"Mally Saint," I say. "She was here."

"No, Mary Elizabeth," Mr Iago says. "I can assure you we would have noticed. Regrettably, Mally has not been here."

"I think she was dreaming," James says.

"Yes," I say, "I was dreaming and I saw Mally."

James knows my Traces come in dreams. He nods to tell me he understands but doesn't say anything else.

I bolt up to stand but thump back down into my seat, dizzy. "I have to go."

"Hey, hold on," James says. "You need to get checked out. You hit your head when you fell."

"I have to go do something. I can't be in here filling out surveys. She said" – I try to keep my voice low – "that Ursula escaped. What does that mean?"

"Twisted," Katy says.

James looks around the room. Everyone is listening to us. "I'm going to take her home," he says. "Let her get some sleep.

142

She needs to rest."

"No, impossible," Iago says, holding up a hand. "An adult will have to sign her out."

"I have to go and you have to let me. Every minute—" I choke on my own words and force myself to my feet. "Every minute I'm not doing something is another minute someone could be hurting your students. I have my internship in Midcity. You can call my aunt. She'll say it's okay, but I need to go now."

I try to calm myself and slowly get to my feet.

People like calm people. Calm people get their way.

"Every minute counts," I say, and look as deeply and earnestly at Mr Iago as I can.

Iago sighs loudly and flourishes with his hand.

I bolt, James right behind me.

"James, you are not to leave this classroom," Iago says.

"I'm her ride," James says, inches behind me.

"James," Iago yells. "James!"

When we get to the car park, the car rumbles and he squeals out.

"You're going to get in trouble," I say.

"I'm always in trouble," he says. "What's new?"

I think of the way Detective Colman made reference to James, like his name was a smear on mine, and the way ever since he was little James never had the chance to be who he is based on his own actions. The son of a drug lord/murderer and the daughter of murder victims make an odd pair, but somehow a perfect one, too. We help each other feel less broken.

Once we're a few streets over, I text Bella. She texts me back like she's been waiting, fingers at the ready, and we agree to meet in Ursula's neighbourhood.

"Will you take me to Ursula's block?"

"Sure thing." He glances at my phone. "You finally going to let me meet your partner?"

"I guess now's as good a time as any. I'm just going to warn you… she's a little intense."

"I like intense. You're intense."

"Yeah, she's more Dreena intense than me intense."

"Can't wait," he says, turning a sharp corner towards the warehouse blocks.

I stare out the window at the faded pastel-coloured buildings, a couple of hardcore Legacies walking a Rottweiler along the street, one with the word LOYALTY tattooed across his bare back. An old man in a bucket hat picks up newspapers from the stand just outside the car, then chooses autumn-red apples and some glitter roses and dumps them in a shopping bag; the boys skating, musicians on street corners, a mime painted in gold so he looks like a statue. I love this place, even without magic. I *love* it, and I'm not going to stand by while it gets hurt.

As we get slowed down by the traffic of taxis, I watch the people gathered waiting for the next bus to come. On the light post there are meeting flyers advertising for Magic Anonymous. "Community seeking courage to accept the Death. It will never be the same," it says, "but we can work the steps and face reality, one day at a time."

Bella's walking in this direction in high-waisted plaid trousers, loafers and a buttoned white shirt, and her hair is in that perfect messy bun again.

"Pull over here," I say. "That's her."

James pulls up right next to her and her hand goes to her holster. Taken objectively, James can be intimidating to look at. He's covered in tattoos and his muscles are tight, not big, but wiry and inarguably strong. I never give it much thought, but he does sort of look like the typical idea of a criminal.

Bella drops her hand to her side when she sees me. I get out of the car as soon as James has pulled over, and he follows suit. I realise as they look each other over, assessing each other, that these are my two worlds colliding.

"Good to meet you," he says. "I'm James."

"Bella. My name… it's Bella."

There's a decently uncomfortable silence.

"Okay, fun's over." I look between the two of them. "Come on, Bella. Time for coffee."

THIRTEEN

BELLA DOESN'T SAY A WORD ABOUT JAMES, BUT I know what she's thinking. I may dress in the same black T-shirt and jeans every day, and I may wear my hair in buns and big Scar-like jewellery on my fingers, but I can fit on the fringes of Midcity as easily as I can blend in here. But James... there's no question where he's from or where he lands in the great Monarch equation. To break through the awkwardness, I start talking about Mally, what we know and what we don't.

Bella spares me a relieved glance for the change of topic. It's not much. We're waiting for the camera footage from the night Mally went missing. It should be as easy as typing the times into the camera system, but we're at the bottom of a very long wait. Mally is still officially listed as a voluntary missing person, and we're forbidden from investigating Ursula, so there's no way to get bumped up in the queue. We're running out of things to do, so we decide to go to the library and see if we can learn anything from Mally's borrowing history. In the meantime, on our way, we can canvass the neighbourhood one more time to find out if Mally has anything going on we don't know about.

Stone is on the corner of Wonder and Vine, sipping on a drink. "What's up?" he says, when he sees me. He doesn't have his bass with him, but he still looks the part: broody with circles under his eyes. He leans forward to shake Bella's hand. "You a cop?"

"Detective," she says.

"You under arrest?" he asks me.

"No. I work for the cops."

Stone nods. "Right, right, I forgot. Well, Miss Officer ma'am, I'm doing my part over here. I have my eyes on things."

"The Scar is lucky to have you, Stone."

"I figure if the Ursula kidnapper comes over here and tries any shenanigans, I can take him down with my board. Whap. Right to the skull."

"Sounds like a plan," I say.

"Yeah, Ursula gave me a place to stay one time when I wasn't doing great with my parents, you know? She's always been cool."

My eyes sting. I wish those Midcity detectives were here now, that they could hear something good about Ursula instead of all the rumours. Of course they probably wouldn't believe any of it coming from Stone. "Thanks for looking out."

"Legacy Loyalty," he says.

"Legacy Loyalty," I say back.

We go into a diner and get some coffee, and Bella smiles when I ask for hers light and sweet.

"You remembered," she says.

"Ursula's apartment is a block from here. Is it okay if we stop by on the way to the library?" I say after we take a minute to enjoy the coffee.

"Uh, no," Bella says, free hand on her hip. "Absolutely not. I can't even believe you're asking me to do something like that after the chief said directly not to." She looks at me, says "Ugh" and then paces back and forth in the sweets aisle. "Bella, she's a child," she mutters to herself. "You can't expect her to understand the importance of rules. It's not her badge on the line. She doesn't even have a real badge to put on the line, so how can you expect her to fathom the gravitas of the situation?"

I want to yell. I want to kick and scream. I'm not asking her to ruin her own life, I just want to stop in and see Ursula's mom and maybe take a look around Ursula's room. I'm about to tell her she has no business calling me a child, when I remember what Tink said about softness and being vulnerable.

"The truth is," I say, "I haven't been able to make myself go to Ursula's yet. I haven't seen her mom or her sister. I've been a coward. The idea of going in her room and her not being there… it's awful. But I think if you're there it'll make it less—"

"Less awkward," Bella finishes.

"Yeah, maybe, or less emotional or something. If I have to hold Ursula's mom up by myself, I'm not going to be able to do it." I've surprised myself by saying something real and feeling it to be true. That's why I haven't wanted to go over there with James. He's as emotional as I am.

"Oh, fine. Fine!" she says. "Just in and out, got it?"

"Got it! Yes, absolutely."

When we push open the lobby doors, I'm hit with a dissonant

jangle of thoughts. This is where I've spent the most time other than my own apartment. Ursula and I are all over this place. Us dressed up for a midnight showing of *Rocky Horror Picture Show*. Memories of Ursula in fishnet stockings and big black boots making phone calls in the foyer. Me, crying the first time James and I ever got in a fight and Ursula crouched down next to me telling me to suck it up and walk like a queen. *Put your chin up,* she said. *Never let anyone see you with your head down.*

"You okay?" Bella asks. "You just turned stark white."

Ursula's apartment building used to be fine, but in the last ten years it's fallen into disrepair. The elevator doesn't work and the mural with the flamingo and the ocean is faded to muted pinks and blues. We trail down the short hallway until we're in front of Ursula's door. I hesitate.

"You ready?" Bella's eyebrows knit together.

"Another minute?"

Bella leans against the wall. "So you've been friends a long time?"

"Since first grade. I changed schools after my family died and I had to move in with Gia. Some of those kids had known each other since they were two. But Ursula came right over to me, handed me an orange marker, and told me to come and colour with her. So I did."

"And now she's missing and you need to check on her mom and sister."

"Right."

"And that's not easy because you feel like this is your fault."

The thought bulldozes over everything else. "I do?"

"Well, I don't know why else you would feel squeamish about seeing her mother and sister. They've probably been waiting for you to come over. So you must feel guilty about something."

I look at my partner, and for the first time I don't feel irritated or annoyed by her. I only feel grateful. I wish I could tell her that, but when I open my mouth, instead I say, "You're really perceptive, you know that?"

"Thank you, Mary Elizabeth," she says, her cheeks colouring.

Of course I feel guilty about Ursula's disappearance, and the truth is I should. I was so self-centred I didn't pay close enough attention to what was going on. And I don't want to admit it, but it's true that she has enemies. Ursula has made so many people angry with her deals and threats.

"You ready?" Bella says.

"Yeah, I think I am."

Bella knocks on the door and then stands back so I'm the one in front.

"Mary Elizabeth?" Morgana cracks the door. Ursula's monstrous tabbies circle the living room behind her. "We were wondering where you were!"

The weight and intensity of the responsibility that immediately descends on me leaves me feeling one thousand times as wretched as I did when I walked in the front doors of the building, especially when I see she's looking even more skeletal than usual. She throws the apartment door open and hurls herself against me and closes her arms against my waist. Holding her is like clinging to sticks.

"Morgie," I say, "are you okay?"

Ursula's mom is a weak woman and is probably not taking care of Morgana at all. If I know her, she's in bed being sick, which is what she does whenever there's the tiniest bit of stress. Morgana's legs jut from a white shift, and she has thrown a black coat over the top that is far too big and crinkles loudly. Her feet are bare and her toes are blue, and inside the apartment the TV flashes against the wall as the cats watch me judgementally from where they've settled on the doormat.

"Are you alone?" Bella steps forward.

Morgana eyes her suspiciously. "'Course not," she says. "Ma is sleeping. Anyway, I'm eleven. I can be home alone."

I touch her shoulder. "That's not what she meant. She was only asking."

"I was *sort of* only asking. When's the last time you ate a proper meal?"

Morgana shrugs. "Ma is home, but she isn't doing very well."

"I'm sorry, Morgie. If you let us look around a little, I promise we won't bother your mom." I give her a reassuring pat.

She clutches herself and lets us pass, then steps to the threshold and closes the door, so we're in the apartment along with the familiar smell of mould and cats and coffee.

"The police said she left on purpose." Morgana roots around in the cupboard. It's almost entirely bare. "Do you want some tea?"

Bella holds up her coffee. "I think we're okay but thank you."

"She would never just leave you," I say. "You know that, right? Your sister would never leave you on purpose."

"I know that. She always said that to me," she says, closing the cupboard and coming to stand close.

"Can I go in her room?" I say, feeling suddenly shy, like a stranger, even though I've spent so much time here. It's been two years since they lost their dad, but this apartment feels like a box of doom right now.

Morgana takes me by the hand and leads me down the small hallway. A space heater groans from behind her mother's closed door, and I'm glad to pass it without going in. Even with the perfect weather outside, this apartment is always cold and wet-feeling.

Bella follows behind me into Ursula's usual mess. Posters line every piece of her wall: bands she loves, #LegacyLoyalty flags, movie stars and comic book covers and pictures of all of us together. Her wardrobe is cram-packed with boas, tiaras, leather, lace, latex, glitter, sequins, snakeskin boots, unicorn onesies and black, shiny gloves, and rows upon rows of chunky high heels.

"Wow," Bella says.

"That's my girl," I say.

This whole room smells of her rose-and-sea-salt perfume. And then of course there's her record player and collection of music in crates along her wall.

I can't be here. It hurts too much.

Bella goes deep into Ursula's wardrobe and Morgana tugs on my sleeve. "Come here," she says.

I leave Bella to follow Morgie.

"Can I tell you something, Mary?"

"Of course," I say.

She hesitates. "If I do, will you promise not to tell Ma or anyone?"

"Sure. Of course!"

"Because I don't want anyone to get mad."

"Okay."

Morgana pulls me back into the living room, away from where Bella and even her mother might hear.

"Ursula. She came last night."

I laugh before I can fully register what she has said. Then I grab her by the elbow. "What? What do you mean? Tell me," I say. "What are you talking about?"

The cats, Flotsam and Jetsam, weave between us.

"She left water in my room so I know it was her," Morgana says. "I didn't see her, though. She was gone before I could. Do you think she's real?"

I think of the dreams of Mally Saint, of the one I had just this morning, of the slap as her body met the floor and the whine of her being dragged across shiny waxed linoleum. Then I remember what she said. That Ursula had escaped and had put everyone in jeopardy.

"I think we can make almost anything seem real when we want it so much," I say. "But I don't know. Maybe."

Flotsam meows as Bella comes back in the living room. She gives me a look that tells me it's time for us to go.

"I'm going to find her and bring her back to you," I say to Morgana.

Morgana holds the door open for us, then hugs me hard. "I hope you do," she says, "because we really miss her."

She slips away, shooing the cats back into the dank apartment.

When the door is closed, Bella rubs my back and I let her. "We'll get them some groceries later. She'll be okay."

"Her mother didn't recover very well from the Fall. That's when Ursula and Morgana lost their dad."

Bella is unreadable. "And now they've lost Ursula."

"Exactly."

"No one has any parents," she says.

"What about you?" I say. "Do you have parents?"

Bella acts like she didn't hear me. "Make yourself useful," she says, ignoring me. "Do something with all your Scar contacts. What about Wonderland? Anything new there?"

I take in a huge breath of relatively clean air as Bella strides ahead.

"Deflection is a defence mechanism!" I call after her. "Don't think I don't notice you avoid talking about anything personal!"

"I don't know what you mean!" she says.

"It could be worse, you know! You could be patrolling with Tony."

She stops and turns round, an unexpected smile on her face. "Mary Elizabeth, you be careful, or I'm going to start really liking you." She waits for me to catch up to her, then pulls something out of her pocket. "Oh, and look what I found."

It's a burner phone, a little black flip. I've seen Ursula with it a couple times but had completely forgotten it existed. "Where did you get this?" I say.

"There's a wall compartment in Ursula's closet. You didn't know about that?"

I shake my head. I never much messed with Ursula's secrets. That was a part of her that was never completely open to me.

"This was also in there." She holds up a notebook full of scribbles.

"So we should turn all this in to Colman and Mahony, right? Do what the chief said and adhere to the letter of the law."

She arches her eyebrow at me. "Well, of course we should."

My heart sinks. "Oh. Okay."

"After we charge this phone and find out what's on it!"

"Oh!" I squeeze her. "You're a genius! An annoying high-strung genius! Thank you!" This is the first time I've felt any hope at all since Mally disappeared, and now that I'm thinking about it, possibly ever.

"My dear Mary Elizabeth," she says, slipping the phone back into her pocket, "that is the best compliment anyone has ever given me."

FOURTEEN

BELLA AND I TRACK DOWN A CHARGER IN ONE
of those shops with phone parts and we hover over it like it's
a sleeping baby and we're waiting for it to wake up. When its
lights come on we're delighted, elated, but then it turns out the
stupid awful secret phone has a stupid awful secret password.
We spend all day trying to guess what it is and can't. Finally,
Bella forces me to leave, tells me to go home and get rest and
she'll call me if she can get it open. She tells me, with cute, smug
assurance, that she's very good at breaking into things.

But something is bothering me, and as much as I try to quiet
it, I can't. The fact that I've tried every combination of four letters
and numbers I think might have meaning, but can't figure out
Ursula's password, depresses me. It signals, once again, that even
though Ursula is my best friend, there's a ton I don't know about
her. Maybe she has a secret boyfriend, too, or a secret cat, or a
secret yacht, for all I know.

Maybe this means I don't know anyone, and that puts me on

an extremely shaky foundation I don't like one bit. I'm sitting on the steps under the Monarch flag, which is next to the United States flag, and I can't move as all the people wrap themselves up to shelter themselves from the cold and move quickly from one place to the other. I'm frozen on the police precinct steps thinking I don't know where to go.

I can't go back upstairs because Bella will throw me out, and if she doesn't, Mona or someone else will. Nights at Wonderland are all about James and Urs and me fighting over who will end with the number-one spot on pinball croquet. They're about dancing to Stone's band and James and Smee leaning into corners and Dally running everything from behind the bar in his white suit and glittering pink-lens glasses. They're about all of us being together, and I can't go down there and do all those things without Ursula because that would mean life is just going on and it can't go on without her because I won't let it.

So, as I explain to James in what feels like a perfectly reasonable tone to me, I won't be going anywhere at all until someone can provide me with a reasonable alternative. James tells me to stay where I am, and then I can hear as he and Smee start arguing about how Smee always gets the shaft when it comes to me. James threatens to throw Smee out onto the street corner, tells me he loves me and that he'll see me soon, and then he's gone, and I hold my phone and keep watching the people walking here, walking there. I'm imagining they have homes to go back to and people they love and best friends and that their lives aren't like puzzles losing a piece at a time until nothing makes sense.

James rumbles up to the station alone thirty minutes later

and double-parks on the curb right next to a cop car. James can't stand Midcity, but he's here, and he guides me wordlessly from the steps into his car. We sit in silence as we drive back to the Scar, and the weather goes from dark and tempestuous to a pleasant midsummer calm.

When we get back to the flat safety of the Scar, the long boulevards and swaying trees, I say, "I don't want to go home or to Wonderland."

"I thought we'd go for a walk by the lake," he says, one hand loosely on the steering wheel, so easy it looks like the car is driving itself. Everything is like that with James. So easy, so laid-back, but under that there's a fighter ducking and weaving.

"The lake?"

"Yeah," he says. "While you've been busy I've been busy. I did a thing with Ursula's ring."

"A thing?"

"Yeah," he says. "You asked me to do a thing and I did a thing. And while I was doing that thing, I got a vision or something… of the lake."

"A vision?"

"That's the best I can do to explain it, Mary. I had Ursula's ring, I saw the lake." He taps on the steering wheel, the only sign of any nerves. "Take it or leave it."

I watch the streets outside as we inch closer to my apartment. It feels like even though James is right here he's also far away. I don't like that feeling. Maybe I'm making it up. It's not like he hasn't been here.

But everyone has these bits of themselves that are hidden in shadow, personal, or too tender to show. Or maybe just too scary.

"I don't know her password." By admitting this I'm showing him one of those scary things, that I may not have the claim on Ursula that I thought I did.

"What are you talking about?"

"I don't know her password. Ursula. Bella and I found a phone and it's locked and I don't know what the password is. Just four numbers or letters and I don't know it. I can't figure it out. I thought I knew everything important there was to know about Ursula, but I was dead wrong."

James puts his hand over mine. "It's going to be okay. Life gets crazy sometimes like you're being squeezed by some giant snake, but then it eases up."

"When you've been digested?"

"Yeah, maybe." He pulls into the lakeside car park, gets out and opens my door.

I thread my arm through his as we weave between parked cars. James suddenly stops cold. "Hey, you see that?"

I see nothing except the lights by the lake and the red phone by the giant sign that says, IN DESPAIR? CALL THE MONARCH 24-HOUR HELP LINE!

James goes over to a white car with dents in it. "Look," he says.

The car is blackened with markings like double Os.

James follows the path to the next car. "There's more of them over here."

It's true. The markings go all the way down the line of cars. We follow them right to the lake, then look at each other wordlessly.

"Whatever made those marks came right up to the edge."

There are signs all around us, all different sorts, but the most terrifying are the ones asking people to report anyone leaping into the lake, to hit the red buttons they have set up everywhere if anyone jumps the rail. Whatever it was definitely went into the lake.

James drops a couple coins into a hat as we pass a man sitting under a tree. "You seen anything out here?"

"You mean the sea monster?" the man says, with more than a slight slur. "Couple times today, once last night. She comes and goes."

James and I meet eyes. "She?" he says.

"Yeah. It's definitely a she."

"Okay, thanks."

"You two take care, now. Don't go falling in the lake!" He cackles until his cackle turns into a cough, and we leave him there, coughing violently.

"James, you're thinking something. What are you thinking?"

He furrows his brow. "Nothing. That guy's wasted. I don't know. I'm not thinking anything." But he's staring at the lake with new intensity and has a tight hold on my hand.

"I want to try something, okay? Don't freak out." James checks to make sure there's no one around. Then he raises one hand and the blue light dances off his fingertips. It glows from his eyelids.

"James," I whisper, but he's utterly focused on the water. Within seconds there's a splash. Something wet and slick and black surfaces and then disappears again.

We look at each other, still. "Something is alive in there." I whisper this impossibility to convince myself it's true. But it can't be.

"Something sure is." He holds his hands out in front of him. Blue light weaves its way to the water.

"James, be careful." The water is deadly and the blue light is connected to James. I don't know if it conducts like electricity or something, but if it does James could be in real danger. We've all seen pictures of how people disintegrate when they come into contact with Miracle Lake. By the time they're fully submerged there's nothing left of them. The fact that there's anything alive in there at all is… well, a miracle.

"Come out, come out, wherever you are," James singsongs into the night.

The blue light dips into the water. Nothing happens for a minute or two, but then a head emerges up to its eyes. The hair is a slicked back blonde, the eyes hard to see in the dark, but I already know who it is and she is looking my way. She's not happy to see me, and by the time her head is fully above water I can say her name.

"Ursula," I choke out.

James puts one arm out protectively, the other one still managing the light. He looks to be somewhere between horrified and relieved. Because Ursula is alive. She is 100 per cent completely alive.

"Stop it," she says, when she's out to her torso. "I'll do it myself. No need to bully me."

James pulls the light back and everything goes dark around us. For a second I think I imagined the whole thing and that Ursula's gone or she was never there and I just wanted to see her so badly I hallucinated. But then there's the sloshing of water being displaced as she climbs over the edge of the lake, water dripping off her, sizzling as it hits the pavement.

She has tentacles, black ones that look to be part of a backless dress. She smiles and then makes a quick motion from feet to head and the tentacles disappear. It's Ursula again, with legs, dry like she was never in the lake, beautiful as always. My best friend, right in front of me. I reach out to touch her. She's cold but she's real.

It's only then I realise I never thought this day would come, that even though I wanted to hope, I was sure Ursula would be taken like my family and would be returned to me lifeless in a box if ever at all.

"What you been up to these days, Jamie?" Ursula says, casting a disdainful glance at the blue light. "Playing with other people's toys?"

"I could say the same to you, couldn't I?" James retracts the light and for several seconds there are nothing but shadows. My vision finally adjusts and I find James and Ursula staring at each other, communicating in silent riddles while I try to catch my breath and to accept the three of us are back together again.

That's not quite right.

We're back together again, but we're not the same. James has this blue light and Ursula has tentacles and I'm the only one being left behind. It's strangely comforting to know that all the fears and anxieties I've been having lately have amounted to something. Things are changing and now I have the evidence before me.

"Where have you been?" I say.

"Here, there, and everywhere," she responds, grinning. "But now I'm going nowhere fast."

I step towards her, but the severity of her glare stops me. It's like she's not even glad to see me. "Ursula, did you know everyone's looking for you? Did you know your mom and Morgana are going out of their minds? I have been completely freaked out… We both have! Even Smee and the boys have been looking for you everywhere. We thought you were dead or kidnapped or—"

"What happened to you?" James demands. "Where have you been?"

She looks at both of us coolly. "I'm glad to know I've been missed, and I suppose I can forgive you for dragging me out of my repose."

"Reposing? That's what you were doing? In Miracle Lake? How is that even possible?" What I really want to say is, *Who are you? Where is my best friend?* Because I'm screeching, but I can't stop. Because Ursula is right in front of me. Except she's not.

"A little old lake is no match for me," Ursula says.

"It's poison," I bluster. "It… It kills people."

"Exactly. It kills *people*."

"Oh, so you're not a person anymore?"

She shrugs. "Call it whatever you like. Miracle Lake is like sunlight on plant leaves for me. It's feeding what needs to be fed."

"Come home, Urs." I'm trying to break through to the person I've always known, but it seems like there's too little of her left to register my appeal.

"There's no home for me anymore, not until the Scar is back to its old self. I have to go back and see this through."

"Back? What are you talking about? Back where?"

I'm desperate, but James doesn't seem surprised by anything she's saying. He snorts lightly, a sign of disgust.

"You want me to pretend none of this ever happened? I can't. That me doesn't exist anymore." Ursula flops an arm over my shoulder. "You want to help me, Mary? Make the city stop investigating. Make the kids at school stop looking for me, make everyone forget about me. Go back to normal and let me handle my business."

"Go back to normal… without you?" This is an impossibility.

"I left a letter in Ma's room and she hasn't found it," Ursula goes on as if she hasn't heard me. "I wanted to give one to you, Mary, but there's always someone awake at your apartment. So inconvenient. But now here you are! It's perfection for my plan."

"Plan?"

With a little flourish she produces a letter from the air, in an envelope, time-stamped from California. I take it. It's real. Real paper, depressions of real ink on the envelope.

"Give this to the police. It will prove to them I'm alive and get them off my back."

I try to read it but the dark makes it difficult to get the curling letters to make any sense.

"No need to read it," she says. "It's just me saying the Scar makes me sad and I made too many enemies and blah blah I ran away blah."

"You… you're not coming back?"

"Oh, sweetie, don't worry, you'll see me again soon. Just not yet. I have people to see, things to do. And I have to go back. I'm not done there yet." She chucks me on the chin. "You need to trust I'm where I want to be and everything is amazing."

"Amazing?" My heart feels like it's cracking in half and I choke out the last syllable. James, who has been mostly silent, touches my elbow so I know he's there. "Amazing? It hasn't been amazing here. It's been terrifying, worse than anything. I thought you were being tortured. I thought—"

"I was," she says nonchalantly, but I hear pain in her voice, and she won't meet my eyes. These are the first signs of the Ursula I know, the *real* Ursula that only comes out when she's safe. "I went by choice and they did their experiments, and then they wouldn't let me leave. It hurt to get these tentacles. And then they took my soul and it hurt so much more I thought I would die. Really I did. But in the end that's when I became free. No more troubling thoughts and pesky emotions. No more worrying about anyone. You should try it, Mary."

"But you escaped from wherever you were. You came here, right next to my apartment. People have seen you. There were tentacle marks all over the cars. That's a cry for help."

She lets out a loud belly laugh. "Is that what you think? A cry for help?" She laughs again, hanging on to the fence for support, then wipes at her eyes. "No, no," she says. "I was just having a little fun, shaking things up." She scowls, going deadly serious. "I'm coming for Monarch, and soon. I just wanted to let everyone have a little fun before I crush them."

"What do you have planned?" James says. "Maybe me and the boys want in."

Ursula considers this. "Maybe later. I'm not ready yet. I have to go back for more."

"More what? Power? Strength?"

"More magic, baby," she says. She changes from a human to an eel to a giant floating jellyfish and back to a human in a matter of seconds, so fast I could almost have missed it.

"Shape shifter," James says.

"Jealous? Not happy with your little baby-blue light?" Ursula retorts. "You want to know why I'm here? I needed to let them know if I came back it would be on my terms. They can't keep me against my will. If they want me around they're going to have to play my game my way."

"Is that what this is?" James says. "A game? Seems like a game only crazy people would play."

"Oh, Jamie," she says. "It's all a game." She turns to me. "I'm sorry this upsets you. I really don't want you to be upset. I know I had big feelings for you. I loved you."

"Loved? Past tense?"

"Look out for Ma and Morgie and the cats until I can get back, will you? Make sure Ma gets to her appointments and Morgie eats, otherwise they're both liable to die." She says it like it's nothing, like she would be okay if that's what happened.

I stare at her, but the staring only makes it worse. She's being serious.

I try one last time to reach her wherever she is. Her soul can't really be gone. It can't be separated from the body, can it? It has to be in there somewhere. "What happened to finishing high school, opening a real business online, making money, buying a house? And mostly helping to fix the Scar. Where are you going?"

She takes my hands in her clammy palms. Ursula, who has always run hot, has hands like cold, damp washcloths. "I *am* trying to fix the Scar. Stop looking for me. Stop looking for Mally. Just stop. You'll end up dealing the Scar a death blow if you don't."

Ursula's still so stunning, round and full as a peach, but she's not my Ursula anymore.

"Don't leave," I plead.

166

"You don't think you're just leaving." James pushes his way between us.

"Don't go." It feels like she's already gone, like the ache of the last few days is going to grow into a chasm as bottomless as Miracle Lake.

"Ursula!" James shouts.

"See you on the flip side, Mary. I'll be back for my mother, my sister, for you, and for the Scar." Ursula launches herself gracefully into the water, feet turned to tentacles. We hear a few splashes and then we're left only with each other and the silence of Miracle Lake, its surface smooth as beach glass.

And just like that, I know Ursula's password.

FIFTEEN

IT'S ALMOST A LETDOWN WHEN I FIND OUT I'M
right about the password.

SCAR.

I had thought of birthdays and people, but it was just this
simple. The Scar is the thing that means the most to her. What we
find inside the phone makes me forget all about Ursula's claims
of not having a soul and of making things right for the Scar. It
makes me forget that she loves a place above all the people in her
life. When we begin to scroll through the messages it's like the
door to Ursula's inner life is opened and black tar is pouring out
all over everything.

There are so many text messages. It's only eight o'clock on a
Tuesday morning, and there's no way I'm going to school today
with everything going on. Bella and I have already spent a couple
hours at my kitchen table drinking coffee, sifting through her
messages, matching them up to the numbers and names in the
phone.

From what we've gathered so far, it seems there were the smaller deals, like doing history papers for people and taking revenge on behalf of broken hearts. That's what I witnessed her doing at school, at Wonderland, taking selfies and collecting promises. It seemed harmless enough, like something she had to do to keep her mother and Morgana safe.

But then, hidden from everyone, even James, even me, there was this phone. And this was where the real stuff was happening. Bigger business deals, brokering hardcore vengeance, blackmailing everyone she could get dirt on. The fact that I know Ursula's alive at least alleviates some of my fears. She had her fingers in so many pies that if we had got into this phone without seeing her first, I couldn't have been convinced she was anything but dead.

And now, the letter she gave me is burning through my pocket. I haven't delivered it to Colman and Mahony and I don't know if I will, but I feel like the fate of the Scar rests on my shoulders. James, my boyfriend, can conjure blue light. Ursula, my best friend, can shape shift and is talking about saving the Scar. At what cost? That's what keeps going through my head. How far does Legacy Loyalty go?

"You all right?" Bella asks.

"Yes." This is the fourth time Bella has asked me this question in the last thirty minutes, as it was revealed through texts we found on the burner phone that the school board has been taking money from Narrows industrial types in exchange for promises to replace Legacy teachers and change the classes to eliminate any mention of magic. Only Ursula's chokehold on three of the school board members has kept it from going

169

through and permanently undoing Monarch High's tradition of acknowledging and respecting the Scar's past. Seeing what Ursula has been up to is hard to stomach, but it's also better to know the truth, to swallow it like a dry pill. But I bet if people find out what a sixteen-year-old girl has been up to, and that this same girl has supposedly taken off to California, they wouldn't let her go gently. She would have a lot to answer for. I'm juggling hot potatoes and have no idea where they'll land.

"Because if you feel like it's too much, and it would be too much for anyone—" Bella starts.

"It is not too much." I try to focus on the here and now and what can be done with the information we have. Whom do we tell? Anyone? Or do we wrap the phone and the notebook in a towel and dump it in Miracle Lake before anyone can find it?

"Oh, boy," Bella says as I'm running down a list from the notebook.

"What now?"

It's been groans and squeals all morning, so I brace myself.

"Do you know the name Caleb Rothco?" she says.

I get a tremor of recognition but nothing I can hold on to. "No. Why?"

"Are you ready for this?" Bella says.

"Yes!" I lower my voice. If we aren't careful we're going to wake Gia, and I don't want her in on any of this. She would probably lock me in the house and never let me leave again. "What?"

"Ursula was fighting with someone named Caleb." She scrolls. "I mean worse than everyone else. Way worse. In this text thread, he threatened her if she didn't back off, and she told him if he threatened her again she would reveal his darkest secret. Then there's nothing." Bella looks up at me and I feel guilty all over again. I haven't told her about last night. James and I promised each other no one can know anything about Ursula being alive until we have more information. Not Smee. Not the boys. Not Gia. And definitely not Bella. "I have a feeling about this one. I think we should follow up."

"Wait!" I say. "I *have* seen that name before." I flip back a few pages in the notebook and tap the page with scrawls all over it. In one corner it says:

CALEB ROTHCO

CUBBY'S TATTOO

WONDER AND VINE

"I know that place," I say. "It's right by the Tea Party. James got one of his tattoos in there."

Bella's expression is hard to read. Maybe she senses I'm not telling her something.

"Bella, I know what we're doing isn't strictly aboveboard. It also isn't about Mally Saint, and I know you're disobeying direct orders from the chief. I'm selfish, but not so selfish I want you to get hurt." I hesitate. "You've been really decent, and if this is the end of the line for you I can do this without you. I have James. I'll be okay."

"No," Bella says. "I'm too invested to drop out now. I'm convinced there's a connection between Mally and Ursula. I just need to be able to prove it. And if we hand all this off to those jackass detectives they'll get all the glory... whatever glory is at the end of this disaster of a rainbow... and that is not going to happen. I've pretty much had it with the boys club over there. Even with a female chief they think they're in charge, that I couldn't possibly be capable of having anything real to contribute." She folds one hand over the other and looks at me levelly. "No. I'm in."

"Are you sure? Because you can go home and take a bubble bath or something and I can figure this out."

She gives me a sideways half smile. She's reached new heights of cuteness today in a pair of plaid dungarees and a red T-shirt with her hair piled high on her head and a pair of red-framed glasses to match. It gives her a whole new level of fresh brightness. Almost makes me want to change out of my black jeans and T-shirt. I pull an old lip moisturiser out of my pocket and slather some across my mouth. Other than some mascara, that's the best I can do today.

"I don't want to take a bubble bath, Mary Elizabeth," she says. "We have to get it together by Wednesday, remember? That's our drop-dead date from the chief. If we don't make some headway on Mally's case we're both headed back to filing, and even though that may be unavoidable, I'm going to do my best."

"Monday is November first," I remind her.

"Yes it is. The thirteenth anniversary of the Great Death, second anniversary of the Fall," Bella says. "Maybe we'll have found Mally and we can be part of the Acknowledgment along with everyone else."

I know it's the wrong time to ask, but when Bella's eyes go glassy I say, "Who did you lose in the Fall? Dad? Grandma?"

For several seconds it looks like Bella might answer me, but then she plasters on a smile, grabs her satchel and says, "I don't know about you, but I could use another cup of coffee!"

"Which one do you think he is?" I say.

Cubby's Tattoo has just opened and it's littered with good-looking guys around our age, or at least they're guys I think are good-looking. Judging by her discomfort, that may not be the case for Bella. Maybe tattoos on bald heads and covering whole backs is going a little too far for her.

"We'll just have to go in and see." Bella swings the door open.

We're immediately greeted by the accusatory staccato of punk music and the smell of faded incense. A girl in the corner is getting her navel pierced, and on the other side a middle-aged woman is getting a tattoo on her belly. There's a steaming kettle and an assortment of teas on a dark antique wood table to the side, and a huge Legacy flag covers one wall. There's also a sign that reads:

THIS IS A LEGACY ESTABLISHMENT.

IF YOU ARE NOT LEGACY YOU WILL NOT BE SERVED.

THANK YOU FOR YOUR COOPERATION. — CUBBY

It's clean and orderly in here. The surfaces are filled with tattoo machines, ink and needle sterilisers. There's a decent green couch in one corner and a table filled with books. By my count of tables in the room, four tattoo artists and one piercer work at the same time, though it looks like two of them are just hanging out waiting for customers.

A blond guy comes over from the corner and checks our Legacy marks. "Books are on the table if you want anything by me or Caleb," he says. "Joe's designs are on the wall if you think that would be more your speed."

I don't answer, so he looks from me to Bella and back. "You're here for a tat right? I'm sorry if I made assumptions. Is it you?" he asks Bella.

"No, we're not here to get tattoos," Bella says, putting down the book she's picked up. "Though this is lovely work."

The guy looks amused. "So what do you need? You selling something? I'm not doing any more donations. Magicalists, Naturalists, Amagicalists. Too many groups to keep track of. I'm a realist, so let's leave it at that."

"Actually, we're looking for Caleb Rothco."

The guy is about to say something when a voice comes from the corner. "That's me." A shadow rises from the corner and steps into the light. He's compact, with green eyes, no hair and a goatee. He looks to be in his late twenties. The idea that this guy and Ursula were going head-to-head is discomfiting. He's got the same look of determination she has, and the way he strides through the room like he owns it has shades of her, too. Seems like he might have been a worthy opponent for her. He might have really scared her. I examine him for signs that he might also be kidnapping people and keeping them in dungeons somewhere, doing 'experiments' or whatever Ursula was talking about, but unfortunately there aren't any blinking lights or signs revealing him as a criminal.

Bella steps forward and offers Caleb a hand, which he takes. "My name is Bella Loyola. This is Mary Elizabeth Heart. Can we talk to you for a few minutes?"

"Sure," he says. "Have a seat. I just have to finish up over here."

The blond guy who greeted us grins. "Like you have anything interesting to say." He looks at us. "I'm the one you want to talk to. Caleb's the dullest guy around."

The buzzing resumes. Caleb is tattooing a dagger right next to a man's Legacy mark.

As I take Caleb's book of tattoos with us and flip through its pages I very much doubt what the blond guy said is true. The tattoos are beautiful, curved and complex, like pearled webs. And then on the last page: a picture of Ursula and a tattoo I've never seen before, an octopus made up of simple, fine lines running up the side of her left thigh.

It's unlike anything else in the book, and it sends shivers racing over me. Did he do that to her? Did he give her a tattoo and then make it a reality for her? She's smiling into the camera, showing it off. It has to have been within the last month, after Ursula stopped straightening her hair and let it grow natural. She's staring at the camera, staring at me, and she's smiling in a way that can only be described as wicked, mocking, an invitation to trouble.

The man Caleb's been tattooing hands him some money and walks out.

Caleb is wearing jeans that are tight at the hip with a tucked-in white T-shirt, braces, black work boots, leather Legacy cuffs on his arms, and he has tattooed lightning bolts coming out from around his Legacy mark.

"You're from here?" I ask.

"Before I say anything, aren't you supposed to tell me you're cops?"

My heart drops. He knows. Bella is so obvious. We're never going to get any information from him now.

"We're here unofficially." Bella looks from me to him, but

she doesn't bother denying anything. "And only I'm a cop. She's just an intern. Ursula Atlantica has been missing for several days. She's known to have patronized this establishment. We're wondering if you have any information as to her whereabouts."

His shoulders loosen slightly.

"We found your name on a random piece of paper in her stuff. We just wanted to check up on you, see if you could tell us anything." Wow. Bella is playing this perfectly. I can see him being disarmed.

His cheeks nearly get sucked into his dimples when he smiles. "Oh, well, in that case." He leans over and rubs the top of my head like I'm a cat that needs to be petted between the ears. "I know Ursula a little. She came in to get a tattoo. She was real loud and made me take that picture of her, stuck it right in there herself."

I bet this is the truth. It sounds just like Ursula.

"She came in another day asking about a septum piercing," he goes on, "but she decided not to do it, and that was it. Never saw her again."

Bella glances at me. "And how long ago was that, Caleb?"

"About two weeks ago."

"And you haven't seen her since?"

"Regrettably not."

"Do you remember anything you talked about while she was getting the tattoo?" Then I remember myself. I'm supposed to be vulnerable and innocent, so I bat my eyes a few times. "I just wonder what she was thinking about that day, you know? I thought she told me everything, but she never told me about that tattoo."

Caleb's pupils glitter dangerously. "Everything, huh?"

"I mean I thought she did until she disappeared. Now I keep hearing how she had some secret life or something. I don't know anything about any of that, so I guess you're right. She didn't tell me everything." I let my voice congest with tears.

"Hey, you're going to be okay. I don't remember much about Ursula," he says. "Hell, I don't remember yesterday. But I do know how we came up with the design. She said when she looked deep inside herself, she saw something slick and many-limbed. She wanted that on her body. I think she was real happy with the work. That's about it. The rest is a blur and I never saw her again, so I have no idea what could have happened to her. She was tough, though. I have a feeling she can take care of herself."

If I didn't know he was lying, I would be convinced.

"Did she say anything to you about anything unusual going on in her life?" Bella says. "Anyone upset with her about anything related to her business?"

Caleb shakes his head. "We talked about poets and the cosmos and art. You know, the stuff you talk about when someone is giving you a tattoo."

This sounds so much like the Ursula I know, my eyes actually do fill. I wonder if her appointment gave her a chance to butter him up for information. I wonder when she went in for the kill.

"Just one more question, Caleb," Bella says. "Where were you Thursday night, the night Ursula disappeared?"

"I work from noon to two a.m., seven days a week. I never miss."

"Okay," Bella says. "Thank you very much for your time."

Caleb waves us out, but I see how his expression changes as

we take our leave, how he crosses his arms and watches us go, features hardening over his skull, and I can feel him watching us until the crowd on Wonder Avenue sucks us in and out of view.

SIXTEEN

BELLA AND I SLIP NEXT DOOR TO THE TEA PARTY and order some coffee and a couple of cupcakes. Once the drinks have been poured and Bella has sweetened her coffee and added in the cream, she looks at me. I think she's going to say something about Caleb Rothco and the provable lie he told about the extent of his relationship with Ursula and the fact that he almost certainly has something to do with Ursula's disappearance.

"Cardamom rose with lilac buttercream for you," the waiter says, and puts a cupcake of decadent pinks in front of me.

"Double chocolate espresso with a cherry chocolate mousse icing for you." He places Bella's in front of her.

"Thank you," I say.

Bella swipes at the icing, then lets her lids drop. "You want to know why I don't like answering questions? I shot someone," she says softly. "A few months ago. I was with Tony. That's why I was in the office doing paperwork for so long. I haven't been able to talk about it. It was just so awful."

I can think of a lot of troubling things, but I wouldn't mind putting a bullet into a bad guy. Bella seems affected. "I'm sorry, Bella."

"I was aiming for his leg, but I killed him. Tony was right behind me. We had gone to question the guy about a possible connection to some robberies that had been going on Uptown. Poof, just like that. He fell right off the fire escape." She clears her throat. "I suppose I did not handle it well. I've had to prove I could handle being out on the street again, and to be honest, until very recently I wasn't sure I actually could. So I'm trying to get back on my game, but it's been kind of hard." She studies her cupcake. "That's why I was a little... well, not offended... but *worried* that they put me with you. But now I don't feel that way anymore. Okay? I just want you to know that. I've spent more time with you in the last week than I have with anyone else in the last three months and it hasn't been bad." She finally looks up, smiles ruefully, and takes a sip of her coffee. "I just want you to know that in case Monday comes along and that's the end of this."

I hadn't thought that far ahead, but she's probably right. We don't solve Mally's case, we're going to be disbanded. My internship will plod along until the end of the semester and that will be that. The prospect is saddening for more than one reason.

"Thank you, Bella. Really." I take a bite of my creamy cupcake. I remember when Tea Party cupcakes were magical. One of my first memories is of being here and my mother having to get up on a chair to pull me down from the ceiling, where I had floated unexpectedly. It's so comfortable in here with its fluffy pillows and lilting background music, I could almost forget everything else and just enjoy Bella's company.

But then she sighs and I sigh and it's like we both know we need to get back to it.

"Okay," she says. "Let's talk it through. What are we not seeing? We know Caleb is lying and we should probably follow him to see if it leads anywhere. There's a clear connection to Ursula, but we don't know that he has anything to do with Mally Saint. We'll check that, of course, and we can keep searching Ursula's phone for a connection, too, but… but what if they're dead?" Bella says, keeping her gaze steady on me. "What if it's someone or something we haven't even begun to think about yet because we are being too myopic? I'm going to try to get some DNA for both of them, Mally and Ursula. And we're going to enter it into the database and see if anything pops up. There was a trucker who passed through a few years ago, kidnapped a couple of people and then left their remains outside of Las Vegas. They didn't put it together for months because no one had done the DNA work. That way if Ursula and Mally are dead we'll be doing everything we can to discover the truth."

"Ursula is not *dead*!" I slap my hand on the table, stun myself and her with the truth. But I can't sit here anymore and listen to her talk about Ursula as if she's in pieces like the Mad Hatter boxes, because she's not. I sense people in other booths looking over at us, and I don't care.

"Okay," Bella says. "You talk. Tell me what you think."

"I think she's somewhere against her will and I believe she and Mally are in the same place. I believe it's Legacy-related." I lower my voice. "When we find Ursula, we will find Mally, and they will be alive. I'm telling you, I'm right about this."

I wait, but Bella has no reaction except to look pensive, like a person might while reading a puzzling book.

"The point is—" she says, finally, still quiet, without any force behind her words.

"Is what?"

"Is… Okay. We need some kind of break, something that can help us find her. Something concrete."

"So we'll start with Caleb," I say. "And you can run the DNA or whatever. Maybe something will come up."

Bella nods, then gazes outside, where a bunch of guys are practising doing flips while a woman across the street juggles. "What a crazy little place this is." She looks back at me. "I've thought about moving out of the Scar, you know. Plenty of people do it. You know how many of us go west because the weather is more like it is here, but the world is the same all over." She takes another bite of cupcake, chews and swallows it. "At least there was once magic here. There's something about it. The air is just different."

I nod. I know exactly what she's talking about. It still smells like fairy dust, like cookies and campfires. "My favourite part about being in the Scar is that you can almost see it for what it once was. The fairy godmothers, the magical clothes, the animals, the mind readers and being able to bring anything you could ever imagine into reality. At least here there's a little Trace of it. I can't imagine ever leaving. I don't know why I would," I say. "I have grandparents in California, but I've met them, like, once ever. Anyway, Gia and me, we take care of each other."

Bella's phone beeps from inside her satchel and she signals the waiter to bring our cheque. She looks at the screen and launches herself out of the booth. "Let's go," she says.

"We haven't paid yet."

"We'll get the cheque at the counter." She flings her satchel strap over her shoulder.

"Bella, what's going on? You're freaking me out."

"Well, you *should* be freaked out. I just got a call from Officer Mahony. They got the footage from Wonderland for the night Mally disappeared and the day Ursula did, and guess what?"

"What?" My body seems to swell and thump simultaneously.

"They went in and they never came out."

SEVENTEEN

BELLA AND I DECIDE TO DIVIDE AND CONQUER. Since I usually hang out at Wonderland nights anyway, it won't raise any suspicions if I go in and see if I can snoop around. I can't imagine where they could have gone. There's only the front door and the one leading out back to the bins and the cellar. There were cameras on both.

Bella and I watched the footage. Ursula went in sometime in the afternoon when it was already getting busy with the after-school gamer-geek crowd. She walked around, got a phone call, went down the stairs, and that was it. So she must have gone out the back. Except there are also cameras in the back and the door never opened until the dishwasher went to dump the grease later that night.

Monday night was tougher. It was super packed because Stone's band was playing. Mally could be seen walking around without Hellion, leaning against the bar. But then she disappeared into the crowd by the stage and never showed up again. The camera quality isn't great, and with the lights down low and everyone jumping up and down, it's like she just evaporated.

By the time we're done watching everything so many times we're seeing double, Wonderland will be in full swing. Bella tells me to do my best and then call her and let her know what happened. We're running on sugar and caffeine and the thirty-six or so hours we have left until we have to report in to the chief.

It's not until I'm heading to Wonderland that I realise I haven't heard from James all day. I call him, but it goes straight to voicemail, then text him a few times but he doesn't respond. On any normal day that might annoy me a little, but now it sends me headlong into panic. I push through the Narrows, commuting into Monarch so they can say they hang out at the same club as the Legacy kids. They've made a mess of the bar, hanging out in spots usually reserved for Legacy, leaning over stools and counters like the place is theirs and not ours. James isn't playing pool or any games, and he's not watching the band, so where is he?

Dally is in his white suit that's covered in sequins and glows in the blacklight. He's chatting and laughing from behind the bar, twirling his rabbit foot, his smile floating. I wave to him and want to ask him if he's seen James, but that would mean he would start asking more questions, and I'm probably just being paranoid.

I play pinball croquet until my name is in the number-one spot again, waiting until it gets so packed in here no one will notice me searching for doors no one knows about, but the loneliness is getting to me. Without Ursula and James, I don't really have anyone. People steer clear of me the same way they did Mally.

They nod to acknowledge me, but they don't come over to talk.

"Sullen tonight, Mary Elizabeth," Dally says, coming over to me with my Caterpillar drink. He leans over the pinball machine so I have to stop and pay attention to him. Then he hands me some quarters. "Tell me everything, honey."

I put the quarters in.

"*Croquet, my dear?*" the sultry feminine voice says. I start playing, flinging the ball here and there, landing in all the right places, watching the numbers rise. Asking about James is an admission, and Dally rubs his rabbit's foot and looks at me with consternation.

"I thought you had forsaken me." Dally steeples his fingers. "Should I be concerned?" He scans me and puts a hand over mine.

I sip on my drink and keep playing, shooting the ball up, whacking it into the other croquet balls.

"I mean, I knew I would have heard if something had happened to you like the others. But it's *eerie*, isn't it? Like this place is full of ghosts now. Where is our Mally? Where oh where is our Ursula? And then you haven't been here, so I'm just relieved is all. I have this awful feeling we're getting picked off over here in the Scar like mice who accidentally set up camp in a cat colony. Meanwhile *I* could be a victim. I could be next on the list. What happens if I'm walking home one night and someone comes out of the dark and nabs me?" He shudders. "No one would even care. They'd just say I got upset and hurled myself into Miracle Lake, same as they're saying about Mally and Ursula. And why would I go over there, I ask you? With the whole lake-monster thing, even if I could survive it, that's the last place I'd want to go."

I let my last ball fall between the stoppers.

"*Que será será*," the machine says. "*Better luck next time!*"

"Nerves," Dally says. "The nerves are bad these days."

"Hey, Dally, can I ask you a question?"

"Shoot," he says as we walk towards the bar together. The band is on break, so we can actually hear each other. "I mean, not really. Metaphorically only."

"Is there another way out of here besides through the back alley or out the front?"

He twirls his rabbit's foot. "No, why?"

I hate to have Dally and all his nerves worry there's any suspicion of anything happening inside Wonderland, but I have to ask him. "You say you saw Mally leave the night she disappeared? Ursula, too?"

"Well, I mean, I didn't watch them walk out the door if that's what you're asking. I was busy cleaning up the night Mally disappeared, and it was busy when Ursula left, or at least when I last saw her."

"But don't you think it's odd that they were last seen here? Both of them?"

Dally puts a hand on his chest. "What are you trying to say, honey?"

"Nothing. I mean, I don't know. I'm just asking you a question."

"Sounds more like an accusation."

"No, Dal. I'm not accusing anyone of anything." Looking at him, I can't imagine he's guilty of anything. He seems so guilelessly offended. "I'm just asking." I can't tell him about the footage, but I believe he doesn't know anything about this.

"Well, don't ask. It's agitating me."

"I'm sorry, Dally. I didn't mean to agitate you. This place is like home to me, you know that."

Dally shakes off his dark thoughts and beams at me. "I'm glad you came back. We missed you. Now go! Enjoy the night!"

When the music starts up again, everyone lifts their phones with pictures of candle flames on them and they all start swaying in unison. In the midst of all the movement, I scurry down the steps to the side door by the stage, but as soon as I get close to the storeroom door I'm paralysed. I can't breathe. It's like my lungs are collapsing, and I think about Dr Tink and how she said to count backwards from ten when this happens, see if I can slow my breathing, get hold of myself. I stumble away and into the bathroom, into a stall, and fall to my knees just as everything goes dark.

"Hey," a voice calls. "You okay in there?"

I'm on a chequered floor, slumped against a metal stall. This is the bathroom in Wonderland. I don't know how long I've been in here, but I can hear there's still music playing outside, so it can't have been too long. "I'm fine." At least I think I'm fine. I'm not bleeding.

"Okay." The voice is dubious. "But it's pretty gross on the floor, so if I were you I'd get up."

I brush myself off as I get to my feet, light-headed, noting that it says, FOR A GOOD TIME CALL MARY ELIZABETH on the wall, with a number nowhere near my own, scrawled by morons about me or another unlucky Mary Elizabeth, maybe. I make sure my wallet and key to my apartment are still in my back pocket and stumble out.

"Oh, it's you." It's Josey, one of the less-evil Narrows. She's still blurry, but I know it's her from her voice, and because even though she's Narrow to the bone with that standard bob and everything, she's always been nice.

"Hi, Josey. How goes it?" I make it to the sink. My legs are still unsteady.

"Better than you, I guess. What happened to you? I'm so glad you're not stabbed to death or something," Josey says. "My mom didn't even want me to come over here tonight. She would love it if I would just sit at home at our new Scar address and never even leave the house after dark. She was like, 'Josey, Wonderland isn't safe. Those people are unpredictable.' But Lucas and Katy were here and I didn't want to sit at the apartment all night streaming something depressing or whatever. She let me come over when Lucas sent a limo for me." She glances over at me. "Sorry. I don't mean to sound like an awful person, but to be fair, it is kind of crazy lately, with everyone just disappearing left and right."

Now that the world is back in focus, I wish she would stop talking, but I can't help responding. "Are you actually saying hanging out with Lucas and Katy is less depressing than whatever you could possibly be streaming?"

She looks at me sideways and gets some pressed powder out of her clutch and powders her nose. "Lucas is not as bad as you probably think."

"And Katy?"

"Oh, no, yeah, Katy sucks, but sometimes I need to hang out with people and it's not like you're inviting me to hang like they are, right?"

She waits.

I wait.

"And also I can't really get mad at my mom for saying stuff like that because I mean, here we are, and you were just passed out on a bathroom floor, which is, I don't know." Josey reaches for my wrist. Her fingers are warm and soft. She strokes the mark.

"Um, excuse me," I say.

"Wow," she says dreamily. "It's a perfect heart. And you were born with it. You're so lucky."

"Lucky," I echo.

"I already told my mom I want to get a tattoo just like that one, ASAP."

"Why? People outside the Scar look at you strange. They judge you. They *categorise* you." I think of the police reports, how they always specify if someone is Legacy.

"But… you guys are free. You're wild and do whatever you want. And you've got the best weather and the best food and magic gardens. And, well, maybe you're not magic anymore, but you used to be. You used to be able to snap your fingers and make wishes come true."

She waits like she expects me to say something back. "Josey, I don't mean to be heinous, but I'm not feeling very well."

"Totally," she says. "Duh, I found you on the floor! I'm sure you've got Legacy things to do. I'll just put on my lipstick over here and not say a word."

"Great." It's funny, though, when I turn back to the mirror I realise she's distracted me from feeling terrible and panicked, and I'm feeling much better.

"So are you hanging out alone tonight?" Josey says after a few seconds.

"Josey, if there's even a small part of you that's thinking of inviting me up to that dais with your demonic friends, please do not. Your lord commander and I don't get along." Before she can argue with me I turn away from her to stare at myself in the dirty mirror.

Then something happens.

There's a shudder in the reflection, even though I'm standing perfectly still.

I blink. Then I squint. Must have imagined it.

But then my reflection in the mirror contorts, a ripple of a face over my own. The girl in the mirror has high eyebrows, her red hair in a Dutch crown, pronounced red lips, and the craziest eyes I have ever seen in my life, feverish with rage.

And they're my eyes. And that's my face.

I raise my hands to my cheeks. My reflection does the same, then claps her hands together and laughs silently.

I must be losing my mind.

Or maybe it's a Trace.

I wave at myself. I can move just fine. This is happening. This is really real.

"Ten, nine, eight..." I close my eyes and then open them again, hoping that face will have disappeared and the pale, wan reflection I'm used to will be there. But it's not. The same warped version of me stares back.

I feel extremely awake now, all my senses at full attention.

"Hey, are you okay? Are you going to pass out again? Because I could go get someone."

"Josey, please stop talking," I manage, but barely.

"Well, that's not very nice," she says.

I take a fingertip and very slowly place it against the dirty glass. EAT ME, it says across the bottom in white, chalky letters.

I am dimly aware of Josey, but it's like she's talking from a great distance, like everything has slowed down except me, the mirror and the reflection that only almost looks like mine. I push. There's a ripple like the top of a lake.

"Do you see that?" I whisper, the fear in me so great I'm not sure I even make a sound.

Josey furrows her brow. "Seriously, are you okay? You're starting to freak me out, Mary Elizabeth."

I push a little harder. The glass gives, turning opaque like silver satin as my finger disappears to the knuckle. Is this what happened to Ursula and Mally? Did this mirror *eat* them?

I pull my finger back and cradle it against my chest. Somewhere in the background Josey is running from the bathroom, letting the door slam behind her.

I'm totally frozen as my mirror image folds her arms and watches, waiting for what I'm going to do next. Then something in me breaks, and I run out of the bathroom and out of Wonderland as fast as I can.

EIGHTEEN

I THOUGHT I COULD COME HOME AND GET myself together, figure out what to say to Bella, and maybe even find my boyfriend, but when I walk in the front door the Naturalists are in the living room and Gia is incandescent playing hostess. I had completely forgotten they would be here taking over the apartment. They're currently sitting in a circle, giggling a little hysterically. There are crystals everywhere and Gia is swanning around making sure everyone has what they need. She's put scarves over the lamps and a piece of black lace over the TV so our little apartment looks like the inside of a fortune-teller's tent.

This is why it's so ridiculous when people include Naturalists in the factions. They're a bunch of middle-aged ladies in flowy dresses on the verge of needing to purchase compression socks, reminiscing because they miss magic and they think if they wish hard enough, it will come back.

There are about nine of them, and each is in an outfit more

sequinned and silked than the next. There are also a lot of hats involved, everything from turbans to fascinators to berets. The women don't acknowledge me and I take the opportunity to try James again, then when I can't get him, I sneak into the bathroom and sink under steaming-hot shower water. I don't even know what happened at Wonderland, but I have to admit that even though it terrified me and the image in the mirror was... well... She seemed crazy, but it felt good.

It felt powerful. *I* looked powerful.

I've just emerged from the shower with a plan to go over to Della's and see if I can find James. I'm trying to make my way out the door unnoticed when Gia says, "Sweetheart, where you going? Come over here and help us."

"Help you with what, G?" I say.

"Why, magic, of course."

The entire circle erupts into laughter. Gia and her friend Ginny lean on each other. They meet biweekly to do psychic testing, try old magical recipes, and spells, and to read tea leaves. Nothing ever works and no one ever cares. This is more of a wine-drinking club than anything else. Thirty minutes trying to bring magic back, four hours commiserating and gossiping and laughing.

"What sort of magic?" I ask.

"We thought tonight we'd levitate." Another burst of good-natured laughter follows.

"Levitate?" I stand outside the circle. "Really?" This has to go on record as my oddest day yet, and I've had some really strange ones. It started with Ursula's phone, then I passed out and stuck my finger in a mirror, and now to top it off, I'm being invited to levitate with my aunt.

"Well, you never know," Evelyn says. She's the organiser with the lists. "Even without magic some enlightened people have supposedly levitated. Why not us?"

"Honey," Cindy, the irritating one, says, "the thing about magic is it's underground. It's running under all of us. All we have to do is figure out how we can invite it to join us. Did you know the entire Scar is built over a bed of crystals? That's why it's so wild here. So let's access that crystal magic and rise up!"

"Come on, baby girl." Gia scoots to the side and makes room for me between her and Ginny. "We need eleven for this, according to the old ways, and we're only ten." She pats the floor. "We already tried it once and all that happened was that Evelyn burped!"

Evelyn reddens. "Don't serve hummus and complain to me. What do you expect?"

I flop down between Ginny and Gia, their combined warm, friendly body heat soothing me. Gia is the kind of happy she only gets when she has her friends around her. It's nice to see her this way, having so much fun and not thinking about bills or money or leaky roofs, or worrying about me.

"Finally," Mattie with the mosquito face says. "I don't have all night. Are you going to take this seriously, Mary Elizabeth?"

"Sure am," I say, and Gia squeezes my hand.

One by one, the ladies link arms.

"Close your eyes," Gia whispers to me. "Let the magic flow through you like a wave."

"G?"

Gia opens one eye. "What?"

"Something happened tonight at Wonderland. I don't know if I should—"

"Shhhh," Cindy says. "You're wrecking the energy!"

Gia pats my leg. "Don't worry. It's just for fun."

"Ladies of the Naturalist Society, welcome back to the circle," Cindy says. She fancies herself the leader here. "Welcome also to the divine magic that courses through our blood and in the ground under our feet. Today we ask that magic be present in witnessing our devotion, and that it bless us with its natural resource. Magic, we know our kind has taken you for granted, misused and hurt you, but we ask you to help us remove your shackles so that you may flow freely among us." She clears her throat of emotion and continues. "Our ancestors carried this magic, and for a brief time we did as well. Return it to us now."

I keep my eyes shut as the women begin to move. I've seen them do this before, so I don't need to look. Each one of them is rotating her torso, humming lightly. When they have done this for long enough, they release one another's hands and the humming grows louder. As much as I think all this is ridiculous, the hum is building inside me and seems to be spreading through my body. My fingers and toes tingle.

I could fall asleep right now. I have the same warmth in my toes as on a good night before bed. Thoughts of good nights lead to thoughts of James, which leads to thinking of his arms, the black heart on his wrist, us breathing together, holding each other, the blue light, thebluelightthebluelight.

And then Cindy is saying, "Nobody move. Open your eyes."

Gasps and a couple of wails bring me out of my daydream. I open my eyes. Everyone is staring at me.

I am hovering two feet above the rest of them. Blue light weaves gently around my waist and arms, like limbs holding me.

Gia's trembling and so am I.

"Mary Elizabeth Heart," she says, staring up at me. "What have you been up to?"

NINETEEN

WHEN I CAN'T REACH JAMES THIS TIME, I CALL Smee. There are loud noises behind him, sounds of a party. James doesn't allow parties at their place and it doesn't sound like Wonderland.

"This is Smee," he says. "How may I be of assistance to you?"

"Smee, where's James? He hasn't been answering his phone."

"What? He's right here. I just saw him on his phone five minutes ago. I was wondering where you were, although I have to tell you, the Cap's not in his usual semi-hostile mood. I'd say he's closer to full-blown." He loses focus for a few seconds as he says hi to someone and I try to hold on to my temper.

"Where are you?"

"Della's," he says. Then, "Maybe don't tell him I told you. If there's something going on between you two I'd rather not get involved."

"There's nothing going—" I say, but the phone signals the call has ended and I jump on the next train over. I don't know why

James is upset, but I do know we need to be together right now. I need him, and it sounds like he needs me, too.

When I see James's car parked outside his godmother's house, I relax a little. I worried the whole way here he would be gone by the time I arrived, but I'm mere minutes from being safely in his arms and finding out why he's been avoiding me today.

I think… No, I know James has never done this before.

The music blares out into the street and the staircase is decorated with people of all shapes and sizes. Inside there's food and dancing. Not many people have their own three-storey houses in the Scar, but Della is an exception. She's practically royalty, was queen fairy godmother in her day, making the best gowns, throwing the best parties, even magicking up a castle when she had to.

"Baby!" Della glides over to me when I'm through the door. I spy a huge table behind her covered in goodies of all kinds. "I've been wondering where you were!"

"James didn't invite me."

She lets her hand fall across her chest. "You go right on in and give him a hard time." Della squeezes me. "Welcome. Try to have some fun. What else can you do?" Della points, her gauzy sleeve opening like a butterfly wing. "James is over there with a couple of the boys. You two ought to dance."

James is by the music. He wears the same overly bright, restless expression as the last couple of times I've seen him. Stone and Smee are next to him and they take off as soon as they see me.

He tries to play it off like he hasn't been acting weird today and leans down for a kiss.

"I've been trying to call you all day," I say.

"I was going to call you as soon as I could get my head together," he says weakly.

"But in the meantime you could hang out here and party and just let me call you fifty times imagining you're dead or something?"

"Well, I'm not dead. I'm right here. I just needed a minute, okay?"

"Oh, you needed some space?"

James and I have talked about how when someone asks for space it means that person isn't into you anymore.

James clouds over. "No, I don't need space. We're just going through a lot right now. After last night, whatever Ursula's turned into. It's stressful. I shouldn't be taking it out on you, though. You're the last person who needs this. I'm sorry, Mary…" He takes my hand. "Come on, let's forget about all of this. Dance with me."

I'm surrounded by people we both know from the Scar, and Della watches us from the corner over a glass of something white and bubbly, smiling proudly. I let James take me into the centre of the room. He slings my arms over his shoulders and brings his body close to mine.

"James."

"Let me talk, okay?" We sway back and forth and I try to let myself fall into him like I usually do, but even though I let myself be moved, I feel stiff. "It's wrecking me to keep secrets from you. There have been so many times I've wanted to tell you everything that's been going on, but as long as you're working for the cops I can't. I would incriminate you and everyone we care about."

I stop moving and look up at him, his warm eyes. He runs a

thumb along my cheekbone. I rise up on my tiptoes and let my lips press against his, let my body dissolve. Then I take a step back. I'm about to ask him a question and everything depends on how he answers it, so I need to be far enough away from him to assess properly.

"Do you know what's going on with Ursula, James?"

The light goes out of his eyes, and he drops his arms to the side.

"Do you have anything to do with…" I press. "Has your blue light told you that? Do you know where Mally is? Is that why you won't tell me? Do you have something to do with them going missing?"

I can't believe I'm asking him even as the words come out. But he knew Ursula was at the lake. He has the blue light. He's been acting so secretive, and he even got a tattoo at Cubby's, which means he might know Caleb Rothco. What seemed totally impossible a few hours ago now appears plausible.

"I'm not talking about this in here." We weave through the crowd, outside and into the garden, where Della has lanterns hung on strings. They give off the same warm yellow light as fireflies, and flutter in the breeze.

As soon as we're outside I turn on him. "It would be a lie by omission," I say. "You promised we would never lie to each other, but the longer this goes on… and if you had anything to do with them or where they are, you have to tell me."

He leans against the railing and looks towards the bridge that connects the Scar to Midcity, and for a second I think he might turn round and tell me everything, lay the truth out between us so we can decide what we want to do with it together. But he doesn't turn round. He stays there unmoving.

"James," I say, "I put my finger through a mirror tonight. Right after that I levitated. If there's something I need to know, you have to tell me."

When he turns to face me, he shoves the sleeves up on his shirt so I can see his new tattoo. *Mary Elizabeth*, it says, surrounded by flowers like the ones in the Ever Garden. "I got this for you," he says. "Because I love you so much I can't think about anything else. Our whole relationship I haven't thought about anything else. It's all been about you, always." I've seen James mad before, but not like this. His voice is usually gravelly and low, controlled, but now it's full of passion, not controlled at all. "I don't know why you can't just take my word for it that not knowing everything right now is better than knowing. I don't know why you can't let me have this one thing for myself until I'm ready to talk about it."

"Ursula is barely even human anymore and Mally's been missing for a week. It's my *job* to find them, and I think you know where they are. You wouldn't be doing this if you could see Mally's dad. And what about Morgana and Ursula's mom?"

"This has nothing to do with that. You know, you've been so wrapped up in yourself, you haven't even noticed I'm always waiting for you, Mary Elizabeth. Waiting by my phone, waiting at Wonderland, waiting at school, waiting for you to remember I exist and answer my texts."

"What? I'm always thinking about you. You are the most important thing in my life."

"No, I'm not. Your internship is. Your ambition is. Getting your way is."

I can't believe what he's saying, and it suddenly feels like our relationship is in peril.

"I go one day without answering the very second you want me and you act like it's the end of the world," he says. "And you expect that of me. You think it's completely normal for me to be that person, not to need or want anything for myself. Well, I found something." He opens his palm and the blue light rises like a flame. "And I gave you a little piece of it because I knew you wouldn't take it from me willingly and it's something you need. *We* need. You should be saying thank you."

"You didn't answer my question, James." I enunciate every word so he'll understand the gravity of this situation. "Do you know where they are?"

He hangs his head. "I guess I really don't matter as much to you as I thought. Can I ask you something?" He meets my eyes. "Do you care about Ursula at all? Or is it just that finding her will get you closer to where you want to be? Do you have a heart, Mary?"

"Answer the question, James."

He nods. "Yeah, I know where Ursula is and I know where Mally is, too. The blue light told me."

Now my dread is turning into panic. My life as I've known it is over.

"What did you do, James?" I say, barely above a whisper. My throat is closing, the world broadcasting its party noises from far away.

"What did *I* do?" He shakes his head. "That's amazing. You think I would kidnap our best friend or stuff Mally into the trunk of my car or something? Did you finally decide to believe all the things they say about me? About me being a Bartholomew? *Captain Crook?* Did you decide to turn against the Never Land boys and me? Is that what you've been learning in Midcity with the Narrows?" He smiles like a wolf, his face widening as he does, showing more of his perfect teeth than I've ever seen, and I take an involuntary step back. "I didn't do anything," he says. "It's what *they* did, what Ursula and Mally are doing for themselves. So, you and your cops can go running around trying to figure out what's going on and you never will because you literally can't see what's right in front of you."

I try to remind myself that this is James. This is the person that up until a few hours ago I trusted more than anyone. And then his face crumples and he comes towards me and I take another step back and he stops, stricken like I've hit him. It hurts to see him like that, but I hold my ground. "I need you to tell me where they are. Before anyone else finds out, tell me so I can stop them."

He considers me, then he looks up to the night sky, rippling with dancing constellations. He returns his attention to me, takes my hand, and this time I let him. He gently kisses a knuckle.

"I don't know how this works yet. But I'm going to find out," he says. "It's going to be a great adventure. And maybe we have some things to work out, but I want to go on that adventure with you. I'll tell you everything if you come with me. You just have to leave your internship behind."

I think about what this would be. James has always been part of the back alleys and secret passageways of the Scar. Leaving my internship behind would be leaving so much more than some filing job I'll probably be back to in a few days. It would mean none of the things I've hoped for myself would be possible anymore. He's asking me to choose him instead of myself.

"I can't do that," I say. "That's the one and only thing I won't do. Ask me anything else. I know how much you've always wanted magic, but it's doing something to you. To me, too. Let's leave it behind and go back to the way things were. Let's move forward towards our dream. Being together – just us, how we always pictured it."

"No," he says simply, as though with that one syllable he hasn't decided to wreck our lives. "Not for anything. Not even for you." He presses his lips against mine and pulls me in close. I would undo the laws of the universe and let all its pieces float just to stay here for one more minute, kissing James. He pulls back, puts a thumb to my forehead, and says, "I'm sorry, Mary."

"For what?"

"Sleep," he says, and blue light shoots into my head.

The world abruptly fades to black.

TWENTY

I WAKE UP WITH DROOL CAKED AGAINST MY cheek, early-afternoon light slanting across my bed, and when I get my phone there are multiple texts from Bella. The night comes back to me along with a huge wave of nausea. I try to call Ursula, then James, and they both go straight to voicemail. Aunt Gia is making a racket in the kitchen, and now I've wasted half of our very last day to figure this out.

I check my health app. Fourteen hours of sleep. Dr Tink will probably tell me sleeping is a symptom of depression, too. I click on the Meditation Melinda app, which I haven't touched yet.

"Tell me everything," Meditation Melinda says.

"Symptoms of stress," I say. "Pressure. Love."

"I see." The avatar on the screen, a woman in pastel pink with terrible bangs, gives me a serene smile. "Recommended five-minute meditations as follows: De-stress with Melinda; Take the pressure off with Melinda; Navigate heartbreak with Melinda. Which will you do first?"

I hit the mic icon. "Melinda, you're annoying. Tell your

creators to think of better titles."

I throw the phone across the bed.

Gia appears in my doorway. "You okay, hon?" she says.

"Yeah."

I'm expecting her to be all over me about what happened last night but instead she just looks concerned, which is worse. Gia's in a red dress, hair all over the place, freckles brighter than usual. She puts her hands on her hips. "Well, I don't have all day. I'm in the midst of cleaning out the cabinets. Are you going to tell me what's going on?"

"Are you okay?" I ask.

"Well, as a matter of fact, Mary, I'm glad you asked, because I am just fantastic." She walks around gathering clothes into a pile in her arms. Gia never cleans.

I feel her forehead for fever and she swats me away.

"No, seriously, though," I say.

"After last night, after what happened... well, it feels just like there was a dark cloud over my life and it got positively lifted away. Anything is possible... anything. And I'm not going to sit around with cluttered cupboards and I'm not going to sleep my days away, either. I'm going to make way for magic. But enough about me. What's going on with you? I didn't even hear you come in last night. You were dead to the world."

"A lot's going on. And nothing."

"Okay... how about you start with the *a lot* and move on to the *nothing*."

I think about what it would do to Gia to know everything that's going on with me. Let her think I've uncovered the magic beneath our feet, and that everything from now on will be filled with joy and possibility. "I don't think I can right now. Is that okay?"

She squeezes my knee. "If we decide it's okay, then it is. So what do we do next?"

"Well, I don't think I can just sit here waiting."

"Yes, I don't see how that would serve anyone."

"I think I have an idea. And it might be crazy, but it also might be right."

"Well, that never stopped you before." Aunt Gia waves me off with her dish towel. "Do you need help?"

"No, I don't think so."

"I've had thirteen crazy things happen to me since breakfast. It's healthy to be a little crazy."

I grab my leather coat and slip on my boots. "Thank you. How do you always know the right thing to say?"

"You know, I spent so many years worrying about you, about your obsession with death and destruction. I've worried that I couldn't protect you. But now I see you can take care of yourself and I'm not worried about you at all. And it's a huge weight lifted off, Mary. A huge weight. Now go! Go be magical!" She hands me my subway pass and keys, plus gloves and a hat.

"You're a good aunt," I say to Gia. "And I love you."

"You know," she says, "your mother would have been so proud of you."

"She would have been proud of you, too."

"No, she wouldn't," Gia says solemnly. "She would have told me to get myself together, which is exactly what I'm doing starting today. I might even go on one of those dating apps."

"That's great, G." I kiss her on the cheek and duck out.

TWENTY-ONE

I BANG THROUGH THE BATHROOM DOORS AT Wonderland. Two girls are sitting on the counter while a third does her makeup.

"Get out," I say.

They all look at me blankly, and the one doing her makeup goes back to applying her mascara.

"Get out!" I yell this time.

"Legacies are the worst." The girl brushes her shoulder into mine, and when they're gone I put a plunger in the door handle and drag the big metal bin across the room, then shove it against the door so no one else will come in.

"Okay," I say to my reflection. "Where are you?"

I stare and I stare and nothing happens. And then I look deep into my own eyes and I think about the blue light and about James and about unlocking things and things not being what they seem.

And then there she is, me, but more malignant and dangerous

looking. I lean in closer to her as the mirror turns watery again. DRINK ME, it says across the bottom. I've heard stories about how mirrors used to act like creepy surveillance tools. Maybe this one's a throwback or something accidentally left behind.

"Tell me where they are," I say. "Show me right now."

The me in the mirror crosses her arms against her red dress.

"Now!" I yell, and in a second she has reached out of the mirror, grabbed me by the shoulder, and hauled me through the looking glass.

A cold wind slaps at my cheeks, slices through my clothes, tears at my open, blinded eyes. The sound is of a howling, of a thousand wolves at once. I can't even scream. If I did, the sound would only disappear.

And then, as quickly as the noise came, it goes, disappearing as though behind a closing door, into a sudden, thick silence. I feel before I see. The air has changed in texture, gone from the humid sweaty bathroom to the cool of air-conditioning. It smells antiseptic. I rub at my eyes.

Blue flashes and it zaps like an electric shock.

My vision returns slowly, from the inside of a tunnel, moving outwards to reveal what looks like a hallway – like a hallway in an office building, somewhere official.

The screen on my phone is alive and well, and still filled up with messages from Bella, but there's no connection. The thing is useless. My breathing speeds up and I force it to slow by counting one to ten and ten to one.

Assess. That's what you do.

So I look around and try not to think about how I got here or how defenceless I am, or even the greater implications of having somehow transported from the hallway in Wonderland to a sort of office cave.

There's a desk with its own chair in a pleasant light blue leather, and a wall with lots of buttons and lights. Behind the desk are several plants all in varying sizes and shapes, placed in a careful configuration. There's a small bookshelf and a lamp in the shape of a leaf.

I swallow against the panic that rolls over me again and think about what I learned in my training. Stay alert, find out what's going on, one step at a time.

And then I see a different kind of chair altogether, if it can even be called that. My heart goes from a dizzying gallop to stopping nearly altogether. The blood leaves my face, my feet, my hands.

I am crouched down behind the desk before I can even totally understand what I'm looking at, or why it's so frightening, its tangle of metal and wood and straps. It's across the room from the desk, in a corner, about six feet tall and made of wood, reinforced and attached to the floor with huge pieces of iron, and there are leather straps hanging from its arms, connected to the legs. In front of me is a notepad – old-style, not an app on a screen. There is also a blue pen. On the notepad are random scribbles across the page.

Screaming, it says.

Pain level, 7

Horns.

I have to get out of here.

I look up, hoping to find some sort of exit. I don't know whether I'm twenty storeys in the air or underground. There's no natural light. There are no windows, and the walls are made of white stone.

The hallway is about fifteen feet wide. On one side it is more of the stone, but on the other are huge slabs of glass, dimly lit from rooms on the other side. The first one I pass is empty, furnished on the inside with a bookshelf, a cot, a lamp.

My breathing has gone uneven again.

I continue hugging the stone wall.

When I come to the next room, the world tilts. There, on the bed in front of me, staring outwards, is Mally Saint. I blink to make sure I'm not imagining things, that this whole thing is not a delusion. Mally's hair is greasy and dishevelled and she's wearing a dirty white tank top. But she is alive. She is alive. Her trousers are brown and institutional. They're also dirty. Food remnants are splattered against the glass in front of me.

I wave to her, put my fingers up to my lips. She is unresponsive. At first I think it's because I'm in the dark, but I quickly realise I'm on the back side of a two-way mirror.

Mally is staring at herself.

I'm so relieved she's alive that all my images of her dead, being dragged across the floor, waterlogged, hanged, strangled, stabbed… they were all in my imagination.

I have to get her out.

I take a step towards her as she raises her arm. Again, I think she's reaching for me, but then her hands continue up towards the top of her head. She parts the dark roots in her hair and curls her fingers around something. I try to see better, step closer, and place a hand on the glass. We're only a couple of feet away from each other and I lean in. Nubs about an inch tall sit on her skull like chunky barrettes. Her face parts into a grin that quickly changes to despair.

"Horns. You gave me horns." Tears streak her face and she stands. "YOU GAVE ME HORNS!" she screams. "HORNS? WHY? WHY ARE YOU DOING THIS TO ME?"

She runs at the glass, hurling herself against it, and slams her fists, continuing to scream, a piercing, desperate cry. Then the pounding starts all down the line, on every pane of glass in the hallways, and it hits me. This is a prison. And as I try to see who's in the next room over, a tentacle slaps hard against the glass.

"YOU CAN'T KEEP ME TIED UP FOR LONG!" It's Ursula's voice. "I CAME BACK! I CAME BACK AND YOU SAID YOU WOULD STOP! HELP!" she screams. "HELP ME!!!"

A beeping noise erupts from down the hallway and I hear the sounds of a door sliding open.

I have no weapon. No pepper spray. Nothing to protect myself. No good.

"I'll be back for you both," I whisper, hoping somewhere she knows.

I run for the wall as the door opens. A high-pitched wail sounds and the banging on the glass stops. It is suddenly silent in the hall.

I feel a pull, like a rope has tied itself around my neck and is yanking me backwards. Open, I think. "Take me back. Open. OPEN!" I say, one last time, and as I do the blue light cracks my skull in half.

TWENTY-TWO

I'M BACK IN THE BATHROOM AT WONDERLAND.
The office prison is gone. I can hear music thumping through
the door.

No. I have to get back. I have to save them.

I face the mirror and wait for my doppelgänger to appear. I
poke the glass. Nothing happens. She is nowhere.

I close my eyes and ask for magic to help me through. I say
please. I even beg. Nothing happens. The glass remains cold and
only reflects the black-and-red bathroom back to me.

"No!" I punch the mirror right in its centre and it cracks.

Then I see her. She's there in the mirror looking back at me.
It takes me a minute to realise it is me. It isn't her. Those crazy
furious eyes are my own.

She shakes her head. She – *I* – won't help me this time.

The train to Dragon Market is empty, just a few stragglers.

I check my phone for the address in Bella's interoffice file and follow the directions on the screen. I turn three or four times down old cobbled streets before coming upon a pink building with red shutters on the outside. The sign is faded but not enough that I can't read it.

House of Fantasia

I double-check the phone again, hear laughter coming from inside. This cannot be it. This can't be where Bella lives. This is a house of fantasy, but even more than that, it has personal significance to me, In fact, if this place didn't exist, I wouldn't exist. Before the Fall, this is where people would come to float, to listen to music that would elevate them. Before the Fall, this was party central.

I knock at the door, mostly sure I have the wrong place. But then Bella answers. She's in a matching pink hoodie and jogging bottoms. This is the first time I've seen her actually approaching dishevelled.

"What are you doing here?" she says. "We're done, Mary. Might as well go have some fun tonight or whatever you do, because tomorrow we're both getting the axe. If you don't mind, I'm not in the mood for any more failure right now. Have a good night."

She tries to close the door but I block it with my foot.

"I need to talk to you. I have to tell you—"

A woman sidles up behind Bella, looking at her curiously. She is in satin and feathers and has jewels in her hat, which is turban-style and gold. She also looks identical to Bella in all but stature. Where Bella is thin, this woman is curvaceous. Where Bella is bony, this woman is luscious. Where Bella is prim, this woman is anything but. She's a vision in a blue satin kimono, feather boa resting around her neck. There is no question whatsoever that this woman is related to Bella, and yet it's unbelievable.

I smirk so heavily I'm sure my lips are going to come right off.

"Bella, my darling," she says, "what have we here?"

"Hello, ma'am," I say. "I'm Mary Elizabeth, Bella's intern. On the task force."

"Oh, sure," the woman says, smiling widely. "I'm Bella's mother, the one and only Fantasia. Well, Fantasia the Fourth, of course, so I'm not the Fantasia from the sign on the door. But for now I'm the only one still alive and I think I'm too old to be having any more kids, so I'm probably also Fantasia the Last." She lets out a belly laugh while I stare pointedly at Bella.

"I know who you are, ma'am." I look up at the sign again. "My parents met here."

"Oh, that's magical! What are their names?"

"It was a long time ago."

"I remember everyone," she says. "That's my job."

I almost never say their names out loud. It hurts far too much.

"Leah and Aaron Heart."

This information usually produces one of two results: horror if they've heard the story, or blankness if they haven't. Fantasia exhibits neither. Rather, she draws me into a soft hug. "Oh, baby, of course I remember them, and I heard what happened. Your sister, too. They were magical, wonderful people and I'm sorry." She lets me go and takes me by the shoulders. "Didn't even die in the Fall. That's no way for Legacy to go. A hate crime like that."

I'm so distracted by her I almost forget what I came for, that I've decided to tell Bella everything I know. I want to ask Fantasia about everything she can tell me about my parents. I want to know if she remembers where they sat, what they drank, what their wishes and fantasies were and what she granted them. Perhaps it was she who granted them attraction and the quiet to get to know each other.

Fantasia sweeps me farther into the house. The ceilings drip with gold-and-crystal chandeliers. The furniture is covered in all manner of good-feeling fabric, silks and satins and leather. Trinkets are everywhere; painted plates from far-off isles, small figurines of women, snow globes. While this house is run-down, it is still grand, and one room appears to lead into the next without end. We stop at the staircase, which reaches upwards more than twenty feet.

Fantasia goes towards the sound of the TV. "I'm going to tell my sister, Stella, to come meet you. We've been asking Bella to bring you over for a nice meal so we could meet you, but sometimes I think Bella's ashamed of us."

"I'm not ashamed, Mama. I just don't like mixing work and home."

"I'm sure," Fantasia says.

"You said you lived in a *boardinghouse.*"

"This is a boardinghouse," she insists. "Now."

"Why would you lie to me?" I sputter.

There's a story in this, but I don't have time to delve into it any deeper, because Fantasia and Stella are back. Stella is significantly younger and thinner than Fantasia, but they are equally beautiful and stylish, and they wrap me in a three-way hug.

"How's Bella at work?" Stella asks. "Tell us everything. Is she annoying? Uptight? Obsessed with the rules?"

"She's amazing, actually," I say. "She's smart and funny and nice, too. It's the worst."

Fantasia beams. Stella pats Bella's cheek. "That's our baby," Fantasia says. Then they both exit, conspiring about getting us to eat a good dinner.

Bella looks after them with a small smile and shakes her head. "I'm not ashamed of them," she says. "But I do like to keep some things private. They can be a little much. It's like the party ended but they didn't get the memo."

At the word *party* it all comes back to me. James, how he did that thing with his thumb and made me what... pass out? I am so angry, but if I'm totally honest with myself, I just want my boyfriend back. No. He's more than that. I want my *James* back, the person who is always there for me, and I want to show him I can be there for him, too. The problem is I don't know if he's even still there. He seemed so different, unhinged in a way I've never seen before, with those eyes, eyes like the ones in the mirror staring back at me.

That was my face, but those were not my eyes.

"Hey, Mary," Bella says. "Are you okay?"

"I'm fine," I say.

"Are you sure? You're crying."

"Oh, fairy dust!" I swipe at my cheek. "I don't know what to do. Everything is terrible." In spite of all my efforts to keep myself together, I am finally unable to stop the current of stress and sadness. I have made so many missteps in the last week and now I'm alone. I slump onto the stairs and let myself sob into my own hands. I feel Bella scoot in next to me, rub my back in soft circles. I cry for so long and so hard it seems like my tears could drown everyone in this house.

"You can talk to me," Bella says, when the tears have subsided.

"You can trust me."

I think about Bella's unwavering goodness. My friends aren't like that. *I'm* not like that. James and Ursula have both fallen off some invisible edge, and I feel myself approaching it even though I don't even know what it is. Yes, I promised them both I would keep secrets, but maybe we need someone who is plain-old good in our corner.

Or maybe I just need Bella.

I take a deep breath to shut out the voice that tells me I'm about to irreversibly betray James.

"I'm going to tell you something that's going to seem completely outrageous at first."

"Okay." I can tell Bella is interested, but she's also wary, looking at me searchingly as though for clues.

"I saw Ursula."

"You *what*?" Bella stands and puts her hands on her hips.

"She was in Miracle Lake night before last."

"I beg your pardon. Miracle… well, that's impossible!" When I don't tell her I'm kidding, she waves her hand at me. "Go on. Tell me everything and don't leave anything out." She stops and points at me. "*Anything*, Mary Elizabeth."

"Yeah, okay," I say. "But you need to let me talk. Just listen."

She leans against the banister. "Fine."

I hesitate but push the words past my resistance. "Well, for starters, there's this blue light. James has it. It's… well, I think it's magic. And I think I got some of it."

She's just watching me now, listening.

"I levitated."

I wait for her to laugh, but she only draws her eyebrows together.

"I know how ridiculous it sounds," I say, "but Gia and all her friends saw. I also... um... went through the mirror at Wonderland and wound up in this office with jail cells. I saw Mally in one of them. She has horns." It's getting easier and easier to say all the things that have been happening. They sound crazy, but they are true and it feels good to tell the truth. "And Ursula. She's the sea monster everyone has been talking about, and she's through the mirror, too. She doesn't have legs anymore. I mean, she *can* have them, but she likes her octopus legs better I think. I didn't know until I saw her come out of Miracle Lake, which is obviously not a thing people can do, but nothing makes any sense anyway. And now James." This is the part that really stings and I shore up against any more tears. "He knocked me out with the blue light. He doesn't trust me because I'm a cop. He knows where Ursula and Mally are. He knows because the blue light told him. And now I know, too, only I don't, not really, and I can't get back. I broke the mirror and I don't know what the rules are, if that means I can never—"

"Okay," Bella says. "Let me think."

"You believe me?"

She nods. "Of course. Why would you lie about this? Unless you're actually suffering from some sort of mental disorder—"

"I'm not."

"Well, then..." She sits down next to me again. "I suppose we need to think."

"Bella," I say, "thank you."

"Yeah, sure. Of course." She takes a minute, head in her palm, before she pops up and gets her bag. "Come on," she says.

"Where are we going?"

"Dining room table. My mom and Stella are going to feed us, and we're going to figure out what to do. We have to present our findings to the chief tomorrow and we are not going to tell her any of this." She glances at me. "And it's in her best interest for magic to stay good and dead. She will shake off anything we have to say about that, especially with no proof. Unless..." She leans back. "Can you maybe levitate on command?"

"No, Bella, I cannot levitate on command."

She sighs as though disappointed in me. "Well, all right, then. Let's get to work."

I hold my elbows tight and follow her shakily into the dining room as she pulls out her notebook and Ursula's phone. She looks up at me. "Everything is going to be okay. There's a pattern here. We can find your friends and fix this, I know we can. There's a solution. We just have to find it."

And even though everything has been so awful and getting worse by turns, when I see Bella settle into the table and begin thumbing through worn pages, I believe she's right.

TWENTY-THREE

BELLA AND I WORK INTO THE NIGHT, AND I eventually call Gia to let her know I won't be coming home. We go through everything in Ursula's phone, including email from a secret address, and we discover through a series of texts that Caleb Rothco isn't like other regular #LegacyLoyalty followers. He thinks violence is the only way to get Narrows out of the Scar, that we need to split off and start our own state. By the end of the night, we aren't any closer, but we've eliminated him as being involved. He did have a secret to protect, but he wouldn't hurt a Scar-loving Legacy. That much is clear. We finally come to the conclusion that we're looking for someone with money, based on what I saw when I went through the mirror. It's someone or an organisation that can afford a setup like that, with glass cages and fancy torture chairs and beeping equipment. It could be anyone from the Narrows, but at least we have an inkling what we're looking for.

My phone has no messages. Nothing from James. Nothing

from Ursula. And although I ache over them both, I'm too exhausted to feel much of anything when I fall asleep in one of the guest beds upstairs in a cloud of sumptuous sheets and blankets.

I dream of blue.

* * *

When we get to the station the next morning, we commandeer one of the rooms and shut ourselves inside. We plan to make a mind map of the things we can share with the chief and show it to her this afternoon, backed with as much evidence as we can muster. We won't mention magic, of course, but we'll tell her as much of the rest of it as possible.

There's one window looking out into a beige hallway, but the station feels all but empty except for a few people typing up reports on computers, so we feel like we have privacy even as the day begins and cops dribble in. We have coffee and bear claws, and I feel semi-normal for the first time in days, or at least busy enough to pretend to feel normal.

Now, without saying anything, Bella hurries to the supply room like she's on rails and comes back with a huge piece of butcher paper, pins, Sharpies. She assigns me to research and print out pictures, then pin them to the board, then she makes lines between the different things so we can show the chief how they're connected.

Bella makes a square around a giant question mark right in the centre of the paper. She motions to me without looking up, as though she doesn't want to distract herself by making eye contact. "So we've got Wonderland, right?"

"We have Ursula and the lake," I offer.

"But we can't say that. We have to just say someone claims to have seen Ursula there. We can say we know Ursula isn't officially ours but since we know they both disappeared from Wonderland…"

"We can probably make a decent case for at least mentioning the sighting."

"Now you're cooking with fire."

I look from point to point, all the little things we have here on the paper, but also what I've seen with my own eyes, the things we can't talk to the chief about, at least not yet. A tremble of excitement surges through me. "Bella."

"Yeah?" She looks up, her hair a dishevelled halo.

"My parents used to have this theory. We have these Legacy markings, right? But what if they aren't just random markings? What if they act like seeds and all they need is something to make them grow?" I spoke truth last night and it felt right. It felt just like this. "What if somebody figured out how to bring magic back? But what if something went wrong? When I was on the other side of the mirror, I saw this chair and there were notations, like someone was experimenting. What if Ursula's tentacles are some kind of… mutation? Mally had horns. I mean, what if they figured it out, but they didn't quite get it right?"

Bella is staring at me with growing alarm.

"Bella, this could be really, really bad. Like, catastrophically bad. What if someone tried to bring magic back, but brought back the wrong kind?"

Bella makes a strangled sound, then clears it from her throat. "I hope not, Mary Elizabeth. I hope you're very wrong."

"Helloooo, lovely ladies!" Tony helps himself to a bear claw and looks over my shoulder.

"Good morning, Tony," Bella says.

"What are we doing today? I got stuck uptown with some tycoon and his love triangle. Bo-ring! He did have a dinosaur robot in his Rolls, though. Should have seen it. He had a special skylight made just so it could fit. These people are eccentric!"

Bella stands to her full height as Tony grabs a chair and flips it backwards, installing himself at the table, running his eyes over the map.

"It's awfully nice to see you, Tony, but we're in the middle of something." Bella opens the door. "Something private?"

"Love the art project." He points to the board. "Are you going to add some glitter glue, because I think that would really give the whole thing a *je ne sais quoi*." He sniggers, then reads our expressions. "Oh, come on. I'm just joshin' ya. I'm sure this is totally relevant to solving your case."

Bella sighs loudly and crosses her arms.

"Oh." He points to the left side. "Is this that monster thing?"

"Monster thing?"

"You know… all the reports of scary monsters running around?"

We both eye him stonily.

"Because if it is, I would *really* suggest not insinuating that's real. Chief is super agitated about riling up the fogies in the Scar with talk of magic being back, and a monster that can roam the city is definitely a sign of magic. You were there, Bella. You heard her."

I look to Bella for confirmation and she nods slightly.

"There was a meeting," she says. "She says between the Magicalists and the Naturalists we could have another riot on

225

our hands if we aren't careful. Anyway," she says to Tony, "A, this is none of your business because it's not your case, and B, we don't need you overseeing our methods. We're just taking everything into consideration." She glances at me. "And of course the lake monster isn't real. You know, I don't even know why I'm explaining myself to you. Why don't you get up off your behind and go do your own work?"

"Well, looky who's come into her own." He slides out of his chair. "I'll give you this advice for free. You should leave fairy tales out of policing. Monarch is desperate for a diversion, and it's so dusty in the Scar all it takes is one spark for the whole thing to explode. Don't get taken in by some idiot who's decent at Photoshop. That picture that's circulating is a total fake."

"Picture? You mean of the suction cup markings?" I say.

"No." He pulls over the laptop sitting off to the side and types into the search bar. "You must have been in a hole over the weekend. This is all over the tabloids." He's right. There on the screen is a picture of Ursula from behind, all curves and legs… eight of them. "Whoever did this has an imagination I can't argue with, though. She's a babe. Wish you could see her up close."

I want to tell him she's in high school, but Bella puts a hand on my wrist, her face betraying nothing.

"Right," Bella says. "You're so right, Tony. What were we thinking?" She laughs, and it's so fake it rings its lie through the room.

"I don't know sometimes. That's what I'm here for. All right, thanks for the snack. I'll be on my way." He pauses. "Unless you girls need anything else?"

"I think we're good, thanks." Bella's voice drips with sarcasm.

"I'm off, then. I have to see about a mistress. Maybe the dinobot did it!" He laughs and then lopes out.

"I'm going to have to take ten showers to get that off me." Bella wipes at her shoulders. "My soul is crying."

"Thank you," I say.

"Don't thank me, *babe*. Back to the drawing board. Time's a-wastin'." Bella taps her watch. "What were you going to tell me when Dillweed came in?"

Bella is back to making lines on the map.

"I've been thinking. The Magicalists and the Naturalists both believe that even though magic is dead, there is potential for it to exist again, if we ingest the right thing or come into contact with it somehow."

"Go on," she says.

"Well, what if someone has found a way to… I don't know, harness magic or something? What if that's why Ursula and Mally disappeared? She said someone was experimenting on her, right? So what if that was an attempt." I shake my head. "It's stupid and a long shot, but I think there's a reason the mirror thing happened to me *after* the blue orb. Like, because I'm Legacy—"

"— the blue light ignited something in you. It was… magic? I mean, Mary Elizabeth—"

"I know, I know it sounds totally nuts. It *was* totally nuts. It was the most terrifying thing that's ever happened to me, and I have had a lot of terrifying things happen." I see the mirror image again, her sickening, knowing grin, her animal rage.

I rest my finger on the box with the question mark inside. "I think if we find the person who is trying to reignite magic, we'll find Mally, Ursula, James, and maybe we'll be able to stop whatever disaster is about to descend on Monarch."

"*If* this person exists," Bella says gently. "*If* you're right about what's happening." She leans back in her chair. "That's a lot of ifs, Mary."

"No," I say. "I'm right. Who is taking Legacy kids and messing with them? Who is making the blue light?" I tap on the question mark for emphasis. "We can figure this out. I feel like it's right in front of us and I can't see it."

The door flies open again.

"Tony," Bella says. "Don't you have a fire hydrant to pee on somewhere?"

"I beg your pardon?"

Bella and I stand so fast we almost knock each other over. It's the chief, donned in a stylish grey suit, her black hair tied in a knot at the nape of her neck.

"Chief, I'm so sorry," Bella says.

She smiles. "I suppose I should have knocked."

"Of course not, ma'am—"

"Ah, I see you're working hard," she says with an indulgent glance at our mind map, which has gone from presentable to looking like a giant scribble.

"Yes, ma'am," I say.

Everything Tony said about the chief and magic and how much she does not want it discussed or put forward as a possibility clangs through my head.

"Well, I'm very sorry to have to put an end to this, but I have some terrible news."

My chest begins to thump uncomfortably.

"We've arrested the Mad Hatter."

"But that's great news!" Bella says. "That's fantastic!"

"Yes, a small-time crook named Caleb Rothco."

At this Bella and I both freeze.

The chief goes on, oblivious to the sudden chill in the room. "Apparently, he's very, you know, anti-Midcity, anti-me. Not the first time and it won't be the last. He thought it would be good fun to hack up one of our informants, as it turns out." Here she sits on the table and regards us gravely. "We are so pleased to have caught him; however, sadly, we have been able to make a connection between Caleb and both Mally and Ursula. It turns out you were right, Mary Elizabeth. Your instincts are sharp."

"Ma'am," I manage.

"Unfortunately, based on evidence found at the Mad Hatter lair, we believe both Mally and Ursula are deceased." She puts a hand on my shoulder. "I'm so sorry, Mary Elizabeth. I know how much Ursula meant to you, and I'm sorry I reacted the way I did, although as it turns out, by the time you had come in here, she was already beyond help."

Bella skitters to me and back. "Pardon me, ma'am, but… did you find bodies?"

For one blazing minute I think I have truly lost my mind, that I've imagined everything, and that nothing I think is real is real. If there are bodies it means I have completely split from reality and that everything I experienced on the other side of the mirror was a hallucination.

"Well…" The chief seems to weigh her words carefully before speaking. "No. We have not found bodies."

I'm relieved, but I'm also something else now, something new and different. Suspicious.

"But you're sure it was him?" Bella asks.

"We have enough evidence to connect him. He knew both girls. He's known to be violent. And he had a kill kit in his vehicle: ropes, hacksaw, trash bags. His whereabouts on Monday and Thursday nights are unknown. He does not have an alibi."

"But that's—"

"And, we found trace elements of Ursula's blood in his shop and on his clothes."

Ursula's blood. What is the chief playing at?

"We believe he got the girls as they were leaving Wonderland and killed them both instantly, disposing of their bodies, perhaps in the lake, which would explain why they haven't turned up." She stands, hands against her thighs. "I'm so sorry again, Mary Elizabeth. Please take all the time you need to process. Meanwhile, we'll be scheduling a press conference for this afternoon. I'm going to get some cameras out at Miracle and on a whole lot of street lamps so this kind of thing doesn't continue." She shakes her head. "It's so difficult, such a shame, but with all the rumours of magic and sea monsters, we've got to get the city under control. People need to be reassured. You understand that, don't you?"

"But that's not enough proof," Bella protests. It seems she's forgotten herself and all her warnings about staying in appropriate lanes completely. "Caleb Rothco may be the Mad Hatter, but that makes sense. He hates Midcity."

The chief folds her arms. "And how do you know Caleb Rothco?"

"Everyone knows him from his tattoo shop." The lie slips

easily from her tongue. She doesn't miss a beat. "He has signs all over that he'll only tattoo Legacy. He hates the Narrows, but he hates Midcity most of all. He has Loyalty flags. It seems highly unlikely that he would hurt another Legacy on purpose, unless he thought someone was a traitor."

"That's enough!" the chief yells, then regains her composure. "We have all the evidence we need to put this whole thing to bed. You can't argue with DNA, Officer Loyola; blood evidence doesn't lie. Please accept my condolences again, Mary Elizabeth. Don't feel you have to finish out your internship. I know it's been an inordinate amount of stress for you. Now, if you'll excuse me?"

I nod mutely, put my head in my hands.

I'm sure the chief thinks it's to hide my tears, but it's not.

She is a liar.

So I hold my head in my hands to keep myself from taking them from my temples and pummelling her with them.

I hold my head in my hands so she will not see my fury.

TWENTY-FOUR

"LIAR!" I YELL AGAIN. "SHE'S A LIAR!"

It's like I'm trying to make myself believe it. All this time I've put my faith and my love and my admiration into a politically driven liar. I thought because she was from the Scar she was like me, that she cared about its citizens and was just playing the Midcity game so she could help from inside the system. That's what I wanted to do.

I should have gone with James, left my internship behind and joined him. I've wasted all my time trying to get close to this woman and she's nothing like I thought she was.

While I rant, Bella seems to be in a daze as we walk through the Midcity park. It's freezing cold and the local children are dressed like clowns, witches, fairies. Here it's Halloween. We don't celebrate Halloween in the Scar. It would feel disrespectful to our ancestors. As I watch the kids run around, I think it's true that people outside the Scar aren't like us and they probably don't have our best interests at heart. They want our sun, our fun-loving clouds, our magical flowers and our properties. They pretend to be like us with their tattoos, because pretending to have magic is better than having no magic at all. But most of all, they want our blood, to cut the Legacy marks from our wrists and take whatever is in them that makes magic grow. But these kids haven't done anything yet. They're just trying to have a good time, get some sweets, pretend life is more magical than it is.

"I never believed we needed magic," Bella says. "I didn't understand why people were so hung up on it one way or another. I always thought the desire for it was a dark path." She slumps onto a park bench like she can't hold herself up anymore. "My father died in the Fall. He was a Magicalist who wanted to restore our family to its former glory. He was at that party the night of the Fall to make a deal and sign on with some investment company. We only found out about it later. He took everything we had in savings in cash and gave it to someone we can't identify because there are no records. And then he died." She glances up. "He was hopeful and greedy and stupid. And he loved my mother and me more than anyone. I miss him every day and I wish I could wring his neck. The fact that he may have been right that magic could come back and that when it does it will be all about money just adds tragedy to tragedy. What's the point of having magic if you're going to treat it like any other commodity? No wonder it's hidden itself away."

"I'm so sorry, Bella. That must have been so difficult, losing your father like that."

"It was. It is. But whatever. That's life, right? It's hard, it's wonderful, it's mysterious." She shrugs. "Becoming a detective means I can figure out some pieces of the mystery, at least."

I take a sip of the coffee we picked up, which is cold now.

"Look, it's the chief," Bella says suddenly, lifting her chin.

I follow her gaze across the park. The chief looks different in a navy-blue pea coat, sunglasses on, sensible flats, less flashy than usual.

"What is she doing?" Bella murmurs.

We watch as the chief follows the path out of sight. Bella gets up and starts walking with purpose.

"Bella what are you doing?"

"I'm detecting," she says. "Come on!"

We have to be careful not to let the chief see us. She checks behind her periodically, but Bella and I are so far back she doesn't see us. We don't speak to each other and try to look like we're strolling, but we're watching everything she does. But all we see, as she enters the bustle of people on the other side of the park, is her edging her way into a crowd and then continuing down the busy street.

"Wait," Bella says. "Did you see that?"

"What?"

"Shhh," she says. "Hold on!" Then, "Look behind us."

I turn round and a man with a dagger tattoo wrapping around his wrist is walking away from us at an unusual pace, even for Midcity. Then it hits me. "That's the guy Caleb Rothco was tattooing."

"Yes." Bella grips my elbow. "He gave the chief an envelope. They didn't even stop walking. He slipped it to her and they kept going. She's dirty, Mary! The chief is a dirty cop!"

My phone buzzes in my pocket as we head back into the park. It's a text from James.

Meet me at Wonderland. I'll tell you everything.

I let that text sit in the middle of my screen like a black hole, trying to decide if I'm going to let it absorb me, while Bella rambles on about the chief and what she was doing talking to the knife-tattoo guy and whether he handed her money or what.

Follow the money, Jack Saint had said.

"I have to go, Bella." I've interrupted her, but I haven't been listening to her since I got the text anyway, so it seems like a mercy to stop her from trying to have a conversation with me. I don't care about the chief. I don't care if she's corrupt or amazing or any of it. I care about James and Ursula and getting to them. That's it.

She pulls her jacket around her. "Go? Go where?"

I think about telling her. I've already told her so much. But this feels private, like something between James and me. I don't know what he's doing or what he wants to tell me, but he would definitely not be happy if I dragged my police officer partner to Wonderland with me to meet him.

Wonderland is packed and is head-to-toe Scar kids. It may not be Halloween here, but it is the anniversary of the Great Death and the Fall, so there are signs everywhere and a bunch of kids are in their #LegacyLoyalty shirts. The whole place is lit up with flashing lights and glitter and feathers, and huge balloons hang overhead while strobe lights flash across the floor. The Narrows are up top as usual, like they don't even know how especially unwanted they are here tonight. Or maybe they do and they're sending Legacy a message that we can't get rid of them. They're still going to hover over us, the boys in over-the-top preppy clothes, the girls in buttoned shirts and pleated skirts, looking so totally *not* Scar.

James is nowhere to be found. I look everywhere for him, blaze past Dally and down the stairs to the bathrooms. It feels like the pounding music and the people all around dancing like it's a carnival have my insides in a blender. I can't breathe.

Ten-nine-eight—

It isn't working and I don't want to pass out in here.

Seven-six-five—

I stumble out the back door in the alley by the bins. The streets are mad. Music is going out here, too, and people pass by the end of the alley, skipping and stomping to drumbeats and the jangle of tambourines. The whole of the Scar is in a frenzy.

I send a text to James, fingers trembling over the keys.

Where are you?

I want to say more. Where are you? Why have you abandoned me? We're supposed to protect each other and you're nowhere. Did you leave me? Did you trick me into making me come here? Why would you tattoo my name across your arm and then vanish?

Do you still love me?

And then as I'm staring at the phone waiting for something, anything to come through, I feel a sharp pain and the world fades out to the sound of a party for the end of the world.

TWENTY-FIVE

REALITY COMES BACK INTO FOCUS IN A HAZE
accompanied by a terrible thumping. There are bright lights
everywhere and my nostrils are filled with a thick antiseptic
smell. I hear a beeping noise and look around. Nothing but
white walls and a mirror in front of me. And then I know. This
is the place on the other side of the mirror and I am in one of
the cages.

I try to stand up, but I'm so dizzy I can't and I flop back down
onto the corner cot. All this white is making everything worse.
There's a beep and the door slides open. I try to run towards it
but fall to my knees, nauseated.

Lucas Attenborough walks through the doors and takes a seat
next to me on the bed. He has something in his hand, grey and
rectangular. "Behave yourself, Mary. If you don't, I'll use this on
you and it will hurt."

I examine it. Looks like some sort of Taser, but unlike any I've
ever seen.

"My dad made it special for your kind. If you try anything it will take you down, so just save us both some energy and don't." He leans back against the wall. His features are sharp and his eyes have circles under them. He closes them briefly, and I almost go for the thing in his hand, but then I realise I'm too weak and he's clutching it too tightly for me to get it from him in the time I could close the distance between us. "Whatever thoughts you're having, don't. You need to hear what I have to say and I need you to listen."

The bump on the back of my head thumps painfully. "I don't know if you know this, Lucas," I say, my voice raspy and thick, "but kidnapping is *not* the way to initiate a dialogue."

He smiles, exhaustion all over him. "I always liked that you have a sense of humour, Mary Elizabeth. You probably don't know that about me. That I like things about Legacy sometimes."

"I never gave it much thought. What you like and don't like doesn't matter to me."

"Fair enough," he says, that Narrows superiority dripping from every vowel.

"What do you want, Lucas? If you're going to torture me or whatever, let's just get it started. It can't be any more awful than talking to you."

He looks at himself in the mirror, then back at me, and lays his hands on his lap, that Taser thing still held tightly in one palm pointing directly at me. "My father made me do it," he says. "First Mally, then Ursula. I kidnapped both of them and brought them here to be experimented on. I thought they'd be drugged, poked with needles, dosed with forgetful serum and then returned home, maybe a little worse for the wear, but nothing more than that. I thought you all deserved to have magic taken from you, superior jerks that you are. I had no idea it would turn out this way, that people would actually be monstrously altered." He swallows. "And now they're all going to die, be put down like rabid dogs, and no one will ever know what really happened to them."

I think two thoughts simultaneously: One, James didn't do it. The relief floods my entire body. Lucas was behind it the whole time. He and his business-mogul, money-hungry daddy. It was just what Mally's dad said all along. Greed round every corner, money at the root of it all. And my second thought is that if I'm not mistaken, he just said everyone in this place is going to be killed. Ursula. Mally. And whoever is in the rest of those cages, which presently includes me.

"I'm an ass, but I'm not this much of an ass. It's all become overblown and out of control. I don't like things to be out of control. I don't mind people getting hurt, but dying? My father isn't going to listen to anyone. He's convinced all this will make him so rich, people will forgive him the collateral damage if they find out. So I'm left with you. You'll listen, won't you, Mary?"

My heart, which was already beating hard, begins to clang dangerously against my chest, but I keep myself still, watching that thing Lucas has in his hands. One thing I've learned: people want to talk. They want to tell you what they're holding inside; they want to get rid of it. All you have to do when that happens is be quiet. Because when you're quiet, the other person will talk and talk and talk. Even though I want to shake the truth from him, we sit there watching each other.

"I didn't know what I was doing at first," he says finally. "My father told me to get Legacy from Wonderland and bring them here."

"Get kids?"

"Legacy kids. I didn't think it was a big deal. But then it all started to go wrong," he says. "There was some kind of mistake." He is quiet then, and it seems the whole Scar is waiting for his answer. "Magic," he says. "It turns out you can't bottle it. At least, not yet. It turns out when you try, it fights back."

"You're trying to bottle magic?" The idea is so ludicrous I want to laugh in his face, but Lucas isn't smiling. Then I realise. The person who could bottle magic would rule the world. And then I don't want to laugh at all.

"Of course we are," he says. "The whole world is in a race to find it and claim it. And what would you do, Mary, if you found out there was a whole lake of its concentrate right there for the taking?" His mouth lifts on one side. It's almost friendly. "Miracle Lake truly is a miracle. And it's not just for Legacy, either, or it won't be. It's going to be in pill form, accessible to anyone who can pay for it. People are going to be so rich, and there's nothing we Narrows like better than watching the numbers in our bank accounts go up and up and up."

He is so settled, so at peace with it. And that is so dangerous.

"Why did you bring me here, Lucas?"

He shrugs. "You were getting too close. Just like James. He and his merry band of idiots were on the trail. That's why I brought him here, too."

I start and he looks at me inquisitively. "Oh, you didn't guess that, did you? He's here and was nice enough to lend me his phone so I could invite you to Wonderland. But it's already too late."

"Too late? What does that mean?"

"It means he's already been given the dose. I had to do it. I couldn't get him to stop fighting. It works so fast."

"Miracle is deadly," I say, trying to fully understand what's happening and perhaps distract him enough to get control of this situation. "It's not magic."

"Miracle is deadly to the skin. It's deadly to the outside. People said Miracle was the blood of Wonder and they couldn't have been more correct. Magic runs under this city, and Miracle Lake tipped us off. Taken internally in micro quantities, that water isn't deadly at all. The bitch of it is, it only works on Legacy so far. That, and we haven't figured out the right dosage. So it's doing something to the people who take it. They're becoming monsters, truly evil. Not evil in the human way. Evil in the magic way."

Ursula. James. What if I've lost them forever?

"How do you undo it?" I say. "Tell me, Lucas. Let them go. I'll fix it and we'll leave you alone and you'll never have to hear from us again. We'll leave the Scar, whatever you want. Anything! Just please let them go."

He looks at me, confused, then says, "You can't. They will never go back."

"Well, then, why did you bring me here? What's the point?"

His eyes widen. "Oh, I thought you understood. I brought you here because I wanted to try a new dose. I think I figured it out."

I look towards the mirror, wonder how strong it is. Ursula and Mally both beat the glass and it didn't break. But I have to bust myself out of here before Lucas has the chance to give me whatever it is. Then I'll figure it out. Someone in the Scar has the answer. The Scar knows magic. There has to be a way. I could be sharing a wall with Mally or Ursula. Can I bust myself through it? Ursula's tentacle only slapped on the glass, but there was so much force behind it.

"There's no stopping this," Lucas says, guessing at my thoughts. "Don't even try. The people in power want magic and they want it for themselves at a very high premium. There's not going to be any solving of this case because they won't stop until they have what they want."

"Lucas," I say, desperate, "I know it doesn't seem like it right now, but you have the chance to fix this before it goes too far. Nothing is doomed yet. I don't know how, but I know this can be fixed. All I need is for you to let me go." I say this as gently as possible.

"Oh no, that's impossible. If I let you go and you told them, they'd kill me. When there are billions of dollars and a global economy involved, not even being a blood relation will keep them from doing it." He lets out a puff of air. "Even I know how I stack up against the power of money."

"I won't say anything, I promise. Not a word about you."

He seems to think about this. His face softens and I think maybe I've convinced him, but then he says, "No. And anyway, it's too late."

"Too late?"

"I already gave you the first dose from the new batch. Let's hope they did a better job with the formula than what I gave James. That one was a real mess." He looks over at me, almost tenderly. "I'm sorry, Mary, for whatever is about to happen to you. Really I am. But you never know... Maybe I got it right this time."

I try to lunge at him, but I'm so weak from whatever he gave me and my pounding skull, I fall to the ground in a heap.

"Give in," he says. "Takes about ten minutes, then you'll be… I won't say fine. You'll be whatever you'll be. It will make this so much easier if you don't fight."

TWENTY-SIX

AS LUCAS EXITS THROUGH THE SLIDING DOOR, there's a quick thump of impact, and his body slumps in the doorway, so the automatic door pushes at him repeatedly as it tries to close. My stomach cramps and my whole body hurts. I retch, but nothing comes out. I haven't eaten since the bear claws this morning, and they were digested long ago.

I try to brace myself for whoever is coming in, but when Bella comes around the corner I almost cry.

"Oh, fairy dust!" Bella says. "This is not good."

"Bella." My voice is strangled. "Lucas…"

"I know. I saw it through the window. I even got to hear some of his villain monologue. It was riveting."

"He… he…"

"Yes, he's an enormous cow pie," she says, hitching her shoulder under my arm to lift me. We exit the room and Bella takes the Taser thing from Lucas, who is completely unconscious.

"Who knows how long he'll stay out," she says. "We need to move."

"James," I say. "Ursula."

"I don't think it's a good idea. We know where she is now. I went to Wonderland after you left. It took me a while, but some girl named Joanie or something—"

"Josey," I say.

"Right. She told me she saw you getting in a car with Lucas Attenborough, and then the pieces started coming together. His father, Kyle Attenborough, has real estate dealings in the Scar. And then I remembered this building being under construction, how close it is to Wonderland. When I got here I could see there were only lights on one floor."

"Bella," I say breathlessly. "We need to set them free."

Bella doesn't say anything, only drags me down the hall towards the exit.

She stops suddenly. "Ursula," she whispers. "Oh no."

I look over to the cage that's just coming into view. Ursula is in a giant pool of water that takes up most of the room. She's inside it, and her hands are shackled by some sort of metal cuffs.

"Ursula!" I shout. My voice is coming back, my legs feeling a little stronger. I let go of Bella and stand on my own.

Ursula lifts her head.

"No," I whisper.

Her eyes glow yellow. I can only see a shadow of the person who was once my best friend. When she opens her mouth, her teeth are sharp and she says, "Mary, is that you? Mary Elizabeth, please get me out of here. I need my hands! Give me my hands!" She pulls at her restraints. That snaps me out of my fear. Her voice is the same as it always was, recognisable as the same one that has comforted me and been by my side for most of my life. I don't care what she looks like. I can fix it if I can just get us all out of this place. We just need to get out.

"Ursula, can you hear me? I'm coming for you."

Ursula grimaces. She lifts a tentacled leg and tries to climb out, but she can't. The handcuffs keep her bound and in the water, hands separated. "I can't move," she moans.

"We're going to help you." I search for a latch, something, anything to get her out of here. "I'm trying, Urs."

"Mary!" Bella calls. "I think I found something down here. There's a button I think opens the cages."

"Well, push it!"

"We need time to think about this. What if she's not... you know... We don't know what's happened to her. To any of them. Maybe we should call for backup now. I think we should have people here before we do this."

I shoot Bella the dirtiest look I can manage. "You're the one who said not to tell them. You're the one who said we couldn't trust them. Who knows what the chief is up to? For all we know she's in cahoots with Lucas's dad. Ursula is my friend. If there's something wrong with her, we can fix it. It's not her fault they did this to her." Before Bella can protest, I call out to Ursula, "I'll be right back, Urs."

"Mary Elizabeth," Bella says when I get to her. She's frozen and speaking carefully, but I can see the fear in her eyes. "I have to tell you something before you turn round, and I need you to remain calm."

"What?"

That's when I hear the slap of something against the glass behind me and I whirl round, ready to attack, and let out a cry.

It's James, his head slowly pounding against the glass. His hands are cuffed with a long rod between them, keeping them apart.

"James!" I flatten myself against the glass, but of course even though our bodies are separated by less than an inch, I can't get to him.

"Mary?" He stops and looks at his own reflection but as though trying to see past it. "That's you? I thought I was dreaming." He shakes his head. "Get us out, Mary Elizabeth. I don't want to go in the chair." He's overheated, feverish with excitement. "No, no, don't get upset, Mary. This is going to be fine. You should see what I got in the exchange. It's amazing what you can discover, left to your own devices for a few hours." His expression darkens. "But locking us up in here was a mistake. You need to let us out so we can get to safety, and then I'll show you what I can do."

"Hey," a voice calls from the next cell down. "If you let us out, I promise you're going to get the show of a lifetime." The voice is measured, cold. It's Mally.

I don't want to leave James behind, so I keep a hand on the glass in his cage and move to where I can see her. Her horns have tripled in size since yesterday. She is wearing the same dirty pair of scrub pants, and her eyes are a swirl of yellow and purple. Her hands, too, are handcuffed apart. "Be a dear and let me out of here," she says as though she's asking for a cup of tea.

Hands. All their hands are held apart. I press mine together and think about James and the blue light and our kisses and the girl in the mirror at Wonderland and I think about going through the mirror.

"Go through," I say. Blue light shoots from my hands into the glass, which dissolves like melted ice and pools at my feet.

"Did you see that?" I say. "Did you?"

"I did, baby," James says. "This is going to be so good."

I smile and let out a sigh. That felt good. Better than good. It felt really naughty.

"Mary, what did you do?" Bella says.

Just then, the door we came through opens and Kyle Attenborough rushes in with two men behind him. "No! They're dangerous."

"Perfect," Bella says.

"James!" I scream. "You have to go get Ursula!"

Then Kyle and his men are on us and I am fighting as hard as I can. And I find that it's a lot more than I could fight yesterday. I kick the gun out of one man's hand and then punch and duck and swerve but feel something hit my chin and something else grab me by the back of the head. Now would be a great time for some kind of freaky thing to happen, like levitation and/or some sort of ability to stick my finger through solid objects such as monumental jerk face's body armour, but I am a total panicking dud right now.

Bella slams the button and Ursula's cage opens. Right behind her is Lucas with the Taser.

"Ursula, look out!" I yell, but it's too late. Lucas has pushed the button.

Instead of Ursula collapsing like I expected, her hands are freed. It wasn't a Taser at all.

It was a key.

I look at Lucas, who shrugs. "I'd rather have you win than him, I guess. You guys figure it out."

Mally and Ursula run down the hall towards the men who are still attacking James and Bella and me. Ursula slaps her hands together and Mally and James are freed of their restraints. Now all of them slap their hands together. Blue light rises in orbs between their palms.

"Get away from my best friend, you morons!" Ursula raises her hands and Kyle flinches. Blue light flashes from her fingertips, and Kyle and his men are slapped to the side of the hall, bound by giant slithering eels. "Be good boys and stay right there until I tell you to move."

"Boo," Mally says. "I wanted to play, too."

"Don't worry," James says, bringing up the rear. "We'll have plenty of opportunity. Come on, we have to go."

When I look up, Kyle Attenborough's eyes are moving strenuously, but the rest of his body appears to be frozen in place and he's moaning.

James's arms wrap around my waist. "Freak out later. We have to go," he says. Then, like he can't resist getting the last word, he stands over Kyle. "You thought you had us beat, thought you could put us in chains and lock us up and forget about us," he spits. "You would have killed us if you could. But you couldn't, because magic doesn't belong to cowards. It belongs to Legacy."

"Let's go." Ursula is beside us now. "I'm not getting put back in that tank."

More men burst through the door.

"They have the serum," Ursula says, and sure enough one of them has a syringe in hand.

"There you go, Mal," James says. "Just in time. Have at them."

She swings her arms out and the men go flying, making hard

thudding noises as they hit the wall. She makes a rising motion and the men get up like marionettes, doing jigs. They are horrified and helpless as their bodies are flung to and fro. "Fools," she says.

"You're magnificent." The words slip out before I can stop them, but it's true. She is really a sight to behold. And I would have thought she couldn't get any more frightening.

Mally lifts her shoulders, standing impossibly straight. "I am magnificent, aren't I?" She brews a new ball of blue between her hands and gives me a small smile. "I like that. Magnificent Mally F. Saint. Maleficent." Her smile grows wider. "I think I'll keep it. Maleficent. I like it. Now that's a name."

The men squirm, making helpless noises.

Mally or Maleficent or whoever she is pokes at the men with beams of blue that seem to zap them. They scream as their eyes fill with terror.

"Aw, it's not nice to play with your food," Ursula says, clapping. "Do it some more."

"Ursula, what's wrong with you?" I say.

"So much." She lets her hands drop. "So much you have no idea."

"Why don't we have this discussion later? Right now it's half past time to get out of here. This way," James says, looking at his watch.

Ursula slops forward, her tentacles sticking. They propel her fast as a spider to a large metal door. She yanks and pulls the door off its hinges.

Then they're gone, into the blackness, all but James, who grabs me around the waist, pulling me off my feet and dragging me into the darkness behind them.

TWENTY-SEVEN

"HEY!" I TRY TO SQUIRM OUT OF HIS GRASP, BUT James is far too strong, and anyway, he's whipping through this tunnel at a speed I could never get to. "Let go of me! Bella!" Last I saw her she was slumped in a corner, and I don't know what Kyle's security henchmen are going to do to her.

"I don't think you want me to put you down," James says. "The spell is going to unbind any second now and you don't want them shooting you with that stuff. You'll be unconscious for days."

We're so far down the tunnel now the light has faded. It's amazing how fast I've gone from being terrified I would never find James and Ursula to being terrified at what I did find. I lean my chin on James's shoulder. No matter what's happening to him, I know he would never hurt me. James comes to a sudden stop and Ursula says, "Now."

James lets me slip from his arms. We've reached a door. As I recognise it, my breath shortens.

"Pull it together, honey," Ursula says, giving me a harsh side eye. "This is not the time for a panic attack."

In the space at the bottom of the door I see flashing lights, and I hear the thump of music.

"We're at Wonderland," I say, trying to keep from passing out with the effort of absorbing everything that's happened tonight.

"How do you think they funnelled everyone through to the lab?" Maleficent grimaces. "But don't you worry your pretty little head about it, because we've got plans for them. Not much else to do in that glass prison besides make plans." She flicks the huge metal lock and it disintegrates.

"Everyone is going to see you," I say, too afraid to touch her but wanting to hold her back.

"We're counting on it," Ursula says.

James kicks and the door opens.

"Stop!" I hear. It's Kyle Attenborough coming round the corner. "We can help you. I can undo this! I just need a little time."

Ursula gives him one chilling smile before she slithers into Wonderland. The screaming begins right away. I can only imagine what the Legacy kids must be thinking, seeing a monster climbing the stairs on suction cups. The flashes of blue light erupt all around us.

James pushes me through and the door slams shut behind us.

"Hurry," he says, "this isn't going to hold them for long."

"James, you have to stop this," I plead. "Listen to them! They're scared!"

The entire club has dissolved into shrieking chaos, and we are part of the tide.

"Get out of my way!" He looks behind him and the watch I

gave him begins to tick. It gets louder and louder until I want to scream to make it stop. Everyone can hear it and now there's just a wave of panicking kids, swarming and trying to get out of Wonderland any way they can. My thoughts are swarming too.

"James, they're going to get hurt!" I scream over the ticking. "Someone is going to get trampled!"

His face stays unreadable and he pushes through the crowd, holding me with one hand, throwing people to the side with the other.

"James," I plead, saying the only thing I think will get through to him. "These are Legacy kids. They're our kind."

This stops him, and he tightens his grip on me. "So soft-hearted," he says right in my ear. Then he rears back and says, "Freeze!"

Everything stops.

The crowd does what they're told. They freeze, confetti and balloons in mid air. And the ticking has stopped. Wonderland is frozen in place.

"Tick tock!" he says, and the music and screaming start up again as we rush out onto the street. He pulls me off my feet and we bound over a taxi and across the street, heading straight for Miracle. I don't even scream anymore. I'm either going to survive this or I'm not.

"They're coming," he says.

Sure enough, more of Kyle Attenborough's goons are right behind us, and James is swaying from side to side to avoid them. I scream as I hear whizzing just next to my ear.

"Darts," he says. "More harmful than a bullet for me now."

We make it to Miracle before the first dart hits him. He groans and lets go of me.

"Stop shooting!" I scream. "If everyone will just calm down I can help. They'll listen to me."

There's a moment of stillness. James gasps beside me. A dart protrudes from his hand.

"Just stop," I say, putting my hand up. "We can talk. We can do that, can't we?"

Ursula has disappeared into the lake, James is standing beside me, an arm slung over my shoulder, while Maleficent has climbed onto a fire escape. She raises her hand and says, "Come, pet."

In a huge swoop of movement, Hellion descends from the sky and lands on her shoulder. It's glorious.

"Pet," she croons. "Oh, my pet. You're here."

One of the men looks up at her, trying to take advantage of her distraction, and before he can do anything she hurls blue light at him. She hits him and he is singed and within seconds has disappeared. Any chance of a compromise or negotiation is gone as the men double down, shooting up at her. Even in the midst of the chaos and noise, she tromps up and vanishes from view, Hellion cawing angrily.

They turn their attention back to me. "Don't move, miss," one of them says.

"You don't understand! They've been missing. They're victims."

"I understand perfectly, miss."

James jerks upwards, raising his hands, and the men pelt him with darts as he gets between them and me, using his body as a shield. My throat is so hoarse from screaming that I hardly make a noise as I drop to my knees.

One keeps his gun trained on me. "Miss, if you move again, it'll be the last you see of this night."

The street is suddenly quiet as some of the men follow Mally and the rest head for the lake, leaving only one behind.

I am focused on James. His eyelids flutter. "Don't close your eyes, James. Please!"

"I wanted it to be a surprise," he wheezes. "I wanted you to be proud of me. I was going to find magic and bring it home to you." He laughs weakly. "They tried to make a magic pill for Narrows, but it doesn't work on them." His laughter whinnies into the night. "It backfired. Mally and Ursula got stronger than them. Ursula escaped. They can't control us, any of us, and they never will."

I let my fingers slip across his lips. "It's okay," I say. "I'm going to take you home. We're going to figure this out and you'll be better and it'll be like none of this ever happened."

"They already would have reversed it if they could have." He is struggling now. "Let me go, Mary Elizabeth. I love you but this is what I want."

"I love you, too," I whisper.

"He's not going anywhere except back in the cage, if he's lucky," the man who has been listening nearby says. "It's true what he said, you know. They have to be put down."

"Put down?" I say, laying James's head carefully onto the pavement and getting to my feet. "He's a person with a life and friends and dreams. And your stupid boss did this to him in the first place. Don't you have a family? People who care about you? Well, he's my family. He's almost all I have and I'm not going to let you—"

There's a crackling noise and the explosive pop of more shots being fired. Something is rising out of Miracle, and it's so huge

I have to adjust my eyes to see it right, but everything else in the Scar stops completely, except the sound of a helicopter circling overhead. There are no moving cars. The street has emptied out.

Ursula is the size of a building and she is slowly emerging from the water, soaking everything in sight. The ground rumbles so hard I have to hold on to the side of the closest building, and the security guard starts shooting, but he's already falling.

"ENOUGH!" she says, and the ground shakes. "Oh, you poor, unfortunate souls. You have no idea who you're dealing with!"

TWENTY-EIGHT

THAT'S PLENTY OF TERRIFYING FOR ME. I HAVE to remind myself multiple times that this creature slopping its way out of Miracle about to destroy everything in sight is my best friend. Maybe she's not in the healthiest headspace right now, but every problem has a solution, right?

Just as I'm thinking I'll be able to fix all this, a helicopter goes careening down to the closest building, where it crashes through some high-rise windows and explodes into flames.

No, not a helicopter.

"That's a dragon," I say to no one. "It's a dragon."

And it is. Not that I've seen one in person, but this enormous flying lizard can't really be anything else. It lets out a cry that pierces the air so loudly, a man trying to cross the street crouches down and covers his ears. Hellion, bringing up the rear, flaps his wings and attacks an officer who has just pulled into the scene and has a gun trained on the dragon, which breathes fire onto the street a couple of blocks away. I hear the sound of screams and explosions as the big glass building begins to shake.

"How is there a dragon? What is going on?" I say to no one in particular.

The goon is hurt and looking a lot less like a goon and a lot more like a guy in need of medical attention. He reaches up. "That's what's left of Mally Saint," he says. "You don't understand. You have to kill them. They're going to destroy everything. Everyone you love."

"They *are* everyone I love."

But I know it's true when I see the horns spiralling from the top of the dragon's head. The dragon that was once a cold, mean girl flaps around above us as Ursula swings her many tentacles until every last one of Kyle Attenborough's men is either dead or temporarily no longer an issue.

"Kind of badass," I say to no one in particular.

Sirens blast in the distance, heading this way. Ursula spins in a circle, and when she doesn't see anyone left to fight, she blasts into blue light again, steps out of Miracle, and gracefully shrinks to her normal size. Maleficent makes one more circuit in the air before descending next to Ursula. She transforms into her human form, horns rising from her head and adding at least another foot to her imposing height. Hellion swoops down and takes his place on her shoulder. Maleficent wastes no time. She kneels down by James and gives me an accusing stare.

"Why did you let them do this to him?" Something about the way she says this makes me want to step on her head, but she seems genuinely upset, and I don't want to provoke another fire-breathing dragon episode, so I resist, even when she runs the back of her hand down his cheek.

"His hand," Maleficent says. She raises it, and where the poison has seeped out of the dart, the hand is turning black.

"Well, get rid of it!" Ursula shouts.

"I don't know how to remove a limb," Maleficent says. "I might disembowel him instead."

"He's going to be dead real soon if someone doesn't take it off. Here," Ursula says. "I'll do it."

"I will," I say. "I'll do it." I run to the axe in a nearby shop window and break the glass, then go back over to where they are. I see it perfectly, exactly where to make the cut on the swiftly shrivelling hand.

Ursula crouches and holds him still. "He's not going to be passed out for long," she says.

I swing high and bring the axe down, severing James's hand from his arm and stopping the poison from travelling through the rest of his body. The black thing that was his hand rolls off to the side.

He screams as I take off my belt and loop it around his arm as tightly as I can. Maleficent magics a bandage. "I'm impressed," she says.

Bella comes round the corner with Kyle Attenborough in tow. "Here you are. I got this guy," she says proudly. "I mean, you guys did some of the work for me, but still."

But I can't focus on her. All I can see is James unconscious, handless, a shell of who he has always been. I can't even cry.

"You're making a mistake," Kyle says. "I'm not the one who should be in handcuffs. They are!"

Ursula is watching him like he is some kind of sea worm, her lip curling.

"You think I'm the bad guy here? Look around. I'm not the one destroying the city," he says.

"You were first," Maleficent says. "You and your greedy friends. We're simply defending ourselves."

"Why couldn't you leave us alone?" I say. "We were fine."

"You were bored and resentful and greedy," Kyle says.

"Shall we?" Maleficent says to Ursula.

"Wait," I say. "You can't leave. Where are you going to go? Everyone in Monarch is going to be looking for you."

Ursula takes my hand. "We have plans. We've had so much time to think about what we're going to do next. They're not going to give up on bottling magic, which means all Legacy are in danger. We're going to beat them to it, make an army of Legacy kids. It's going to be beautiful. We'll be restored to our former glory and everything will be the way it was, only better. We'll all have a common goal. No more high school, no more Narrows encroaching on our territory, no more rules, no more doing what the city tells us to. We're going to be in charge. Instead of being their minions, they'll be ours. We'll make them pay in flesh for every single thing they've ever done to us."

Nothing in the history books ever said anything about this before. The occasional evil wizard would appear, sure, but the citizens of the Scar were basically good people trying to make ends meet and raise their kids.

"This isn't what the Scar is about," I say.

"It is," Ursula says. "Come with us," she tries one more time. I glance back at Bella, who is holding Kyle Attenborough in handcuffs, watching us.

Maleficent rolls her eyes.

260

"I can't," I say.

She drops my hand. "Well, I'm sorry to disappoint you, Mary Elizabeth. I'm sorry not to be some ideal person, but you heard him. I'm not going to let myself get put down. And I'm not going to let these jerks take over the Scar and use us like we're lab rats. We're going to get them before they get us or anyone else."

"That's… evil."

"Their fault," Ursula says. "We're their creation. But I guess you're right. We'll be the villains and you're going to be the heroine of this story, like you always wanted."

Maleficent appears behind Ursula and takes her by the elbow. "Let's go. We don't have much time."

"You look good as a dragon," Ursula says to her.

"You look good as a giant octopus," Maleficent says.

Ursula looks down at James. "What do we do with him?"

The sirens give way to slamming doors and the sound of footfalls.

"Take him." Much as I don't want Mally or Ursula to think I approve of what they're doing, I don't want James falling into Kyle Attenborough's hands or even the chief's. I honestly don't know whom to trust. "Please, just take him with you. I'll find you when it's safe."

Ursula hugs me. "It's never going to be safe again," she says.

And then she picks James up like he's limp seaweed and throws him over her shoulder.

"Wait!" I cry out. I go over to him and kiss his pale cheek. "Come back to me," I say. "Come back."

I feel tears dripping down my cheeks.

You're going to have to choose between your head and your heart.

I understand it now. James is my heart and so is Ursula, and they're both so far from me now I'll never get them back.

With a single flourish from Maleficent, James is gone. Ursula's gone. And they've taken my whole life with them.

"You're a stupid girl, you know that?" Kyle says to me. "You think you just saved the city, but you have murdered every one of its citizens, letting them go like that."

A couple of officers I don't know round the corner into the alley.

"We've got it," Bella says. "Perp is under control."

"Hey, it's that intern kid," the female officer says, eyes bouncing from me to Kyle until she's certain there's no threat. She lets her gun fall to her side.

"Isn't that Kyle Attenborough?" the man says.

Kyle sneers at me, as best he can with his hands zip-tied behind his back. "Magic is back," he says. "And not only is it back, but it is in the hands of the evilest creatures ever to exist. Congratulations."

"That'll be enough out of you," Bella says, lifting him to his feet to take him to the squad car.

Bella tells me she'll meet me at the station to officially book him into custody, and when he's out of sight, I allow myself to tremble as I sit on the curb. The sign to Wonderland is still flashing, and pieces of broken glass and bodies are strewn everywhere. Medics have begun to collect Kyle's men one by one and put some into ambulances, while others are covered in blankets, a signal that they will need to be collected for the morgue.

My friends did that. The love of my life did that.

My phone vibrates in my pocket and I answer it automatically, without looking at who's calling.

"Mary Elizabeth, is that you?" It's Dr Tink, sounding even more perky than usual. I don't answer, but it doesn't seem to matter. "Oh good. I've pencilled you in for tomorrow at eight a.m., okay? Don't stand me up or I'll have to report you. See you then?"

"I think that would be great," I say, looking at the destruction all around me. "I have a lot to tell you."

Magic is back.

Magic is back.

Magic is back.

ACKNOWLEDGEMENTS

TO JOCELYN DAVIES, MY EDITOR, FOR THE excellent mindmelds, for giving me the opportunity to explore and reimagine the universe of my childhood, and for encouraging me every step of the way. You're a dreamy editor. Writing for Disney was something I wished upon a star for many years ago, and it has been granted by you. Thank you, many times over.

Thank you to the team at Disney who brought this book to life, including Phil Buchanan, Guy Cunningham, Sara Liebling, Lyssa Hurvitz, Seale Ballenger, Tim Retzlaff, Elke Villa, Dina Sherman, the entire sales team, Kieran Viola and Emily Meehan. Thanks to Joshua Hixson for the gorgeous cover.

My agent, Emily van Beek, for your constant assured presence and grace. Obviously I wouldn't be who I am without you, and I love you.

My children, Lilu and Bodhi: The two of you are still and always making my dreams come true, simply by existing, but even more, every day, by being the remarkable humans you are.

I got so lucky to be your mother and have you both as my best friends.

My husband, Chris, you're a stone-cold miracle. Thank you for supporting my juggling, my ambition and for listening when the fears get the better of me. I hope I'm half the partner you are.

My colleagues and students at Taos Academy Charter School: You make life exciting and beautiful and you are all filled with magic. I thank you so much for giving me a second home.

My parents, thank you for giving me life and for instilling in me from a very young age the importance of books. You may be responsible for everything that has come after.

My siblings, all the love. #oneofsix

My dearest Nancy Jenkins, who forces conversations about good and evil that make their way into everything I write.

All my friends, writers and non, who make life colourful and adventurous, thank you.

Last, thank you to Disney for imagining a world that has been such a pure joy to play in and such rich characters. I spent my childhood obsessing over your creations, and so this project has satisfied a particular, persistent itch. It has been a blessing and a pleasure and a little bit of fairy dust, too.

I believe in magic. I believe. I believe.